1

He heard us coming and turned.
"Well. Hello, Amanda. Hello Daniel. . ."

He sounded embarrassed, and we were embarrassed too and not just by having a live parent with us inside the school grounds. He was a stranger to us, with a stranger's face. It was long and tough-skinned, with wrinkles in unlikely places. He had slow, dark eyes and he was too old to be a father. Or looked it. Too old to be my father, anyway, I thought.

A tall man with big shoulders, he wore his suit in a way which said he didn't often wear smart clothes. This was a man who had been roaming wide-open spaces eleven thousand miles away and that was what you saw when you looked at him.

Looking down at us he would have seen two kids who were pretty used to being outside too. Rockhill School went in for lots of outdoor activities. It had to, because indoor facilities were limited. It was a boarding school but there was nothing fancy about it. Most of the pupils had parents in the armed forces or came from families who worked abroad, and the school was housed in the buildings left over when the RAF moved out from Rockhill Airfield. Most of the structures were prefabricated – not built to last as long as they had; but the teachers lived in the officers' quarters, which were like regular homes. A few years ago the school had become co-educational, for financial reasons more than anything else, and even then it only just struggled by.

It was summer and the earth was crusty on the football pitch where we stood with our stranger-father. You could still make out the outlines of the overgrown runways all around us. We had been told to go where he was standing looking out over the flat land, and had made the long walk from the dining hall. I remember we missed pudding that day.

"Well . . . you're both OK, are you?"

We made noises which indicated that we were at least alive. I don't know what he thought of us. Dan was small for his age and had his expression set to fully-closed; while I was thin and, to be honest, bony in those days. I was a teenager by then and had been for a while, so I felt infinitely superior to Dan. We were wearing tracksuits which never quite lost the smell of the changing rooms, even when they were newly washed.

"So. Do you remember me?"

You could tell he didn't expect us to and didn't even wait for an answer. He sighed. "Well, it's been. . ."

A long time. We knew. He put out his hand and ruffled Dan's hair, which was a bad move. Then he waited a little while, wanting to say something right, and when he couldn't he said, "Let's go somewhere. I've got a car."

You could see the old Landrover in the street, right outside the windows of the tea rooms where we sat. It was a Saturday and the whole of Derby, and this place too, was crowded. But our . . . dad . . . managed to park exactly where he wanted to, even if the big green jeep was halfway up the pavement. He was impatient, an adventurer. Only it didn't show on his face. Perhaps this was where Dan had got his own "you're getting nothing from me" expression.

So far we hadn't talked much. He had been watching us eat. We ate a lot and not just because it was a treat to get away from school food: while we were eating, we couldn't be expected to speak.

He said, "Your gran's going to be sorry to lose you."

That wasn't entirely true. Our one and only grandmother had looked after us for ten years, ever since our mother died. Now she felt she couldn't cope any more, which was why we had been put into Rockhill while she sold her house and went to live in an old people's home.

Dan was bolder than me. "You're sorry about it. You wouldn't have come back if she was still well."

The challenging note in his voice was muffled by a half-masticated scone, but it still came through.

"I was always going to come back. One day. I'm your father."

Was he hurt? No way of knowing. In case he was, I tried to see it from his point of view.

"Australia must be wonderful," I said, forcing cheerfulness into my voice. "And, um, mining for bauxite – well – that's probably really exciting."

"Look." He was much crosser with me than he had been with Dan. "What I do – did – to make a living – a good living – you can't do in England. All my life I've travelled. When your mother died we needed more money than I was earning here. It's that simple."

We digested food, and digested too what he had just said. Surely there was more to it than that. Neither of us could remember him at all. He had gone away and stayed away.

"It's –" he floundered on, driven to it by our silence – "it's the way things turned out. That's all."

"What do we call you?" Dan asked, taking him by surprise again.

Our father thought carefully. "John. That's. . . I think. . . Well – it's my name. I don't feel like a 'Dad' or a . . . 'Daddy'."

Well, he said it.

In the half-term we went on holiday with John. Dan and I imagined that we would be spending some time looking for another place to live in Manchester, probably near where Gran's house had been. We couldn't conceive that our lives would change to the extent where we wouldn't be near our friends in our own area.

As it happened we didn't go too far from Manchester for the holiday, so we weren't worried yet. We booked into a small hotel in Buxton, in the Peak District. We were only there in the evenings. John wouldn't keep still for a minute – we always had to be doing something. "What's the plan today?" he would say, and then he would tell us what it was and we'd be back in the Landrover, which was old and so noisy you had to shout if you wanted to say something.

He didn't want to talk. That was what it was. Here we were, supposed to be getting to know each other, and it was like he was a tour guide.

We went into Manchester once, and it was good to be in a place where we felt at home. First off we visited Gran in her residential home, a big red-brick house in Cheadle. Inside there was a medley of flower-patterns everywhere, all over the curtains and furniture and carpets, as if someone had exploded several gardens inside the building. Gran was in what they called the morning room, not the room with the big television set.

She looked much older and more tired than I remembered. We had only seen her a few weeks ago and now she seemed to have slowed right down. She was small and slight, as our mother had been. Not that either of us could remember our mother; Gran had been everything to us for as long as time itself. We chatted while John was talking to the matron somewhere else.

Gran said cheerfully, "Isn't it lovely? Having a dad?" and wanted us to agree at once so she could feel comfortable, only we didn't. "Well – isn't it?" she repeated with sudden asperity.

"It's all right," Dan said glumly.

"He's, um, he's nice," I contributed.

"He's not very interested in us, though," Dan said matter-of-factly.

"Well of course he is." Gran answered.

"If he'd been interested he'd have come over to see us – in the holidays. We'd have seen him."

"Australia is a long way away. He wrote letters, didn't he?"

I said carefully, "Yes, but . . . he didn't say much in them."

Dan was enjoying his own belligerence. "He could have got us over there. To Australia. He just couldn't have cared less – that's what it was."

Gran didn't like this conversation at all. "We had each other, didn't we, dears. We were all right."

"Not even in the holidays," Dan persisted.

"Your father didn't have holidays – not like you do. He had a business to start and keep running. And I'm afraid he's the kind of man who thinks he's indispensable wherever he is." She was firm, in the way she used to be. "What he did, he did for you as much as for himself. That I'm sure of. And he's here now and it wasn't easy for him to be."

To which Dan, true to character, made the obvious response. "It's not easy for us, either."

Later we watched the television in the other room. It was a news programme and not very interesting. Looking across the hall, we could see John and Gran talking seriously. To be more accurate, she was talking seriously and he seemed to be listening seriously.

That afternoon he avoided talking to us by taking us to the cinema. We saw an action film about jungle warfare. Dan's choice. Afterwards he asked John about what it had been like being an Army

Captain, which he had been, and John said, "Not like that, anyway," and smiled to himself about the film, which had been the best part of the half-term so far. It was hard to like him and it was hard to dislike him, too; you have to know someone to like or dislike them.

We were getting to know the Peak District, though. Gradually we were driving farther every day, stopping the car and walking for miles. The wilder the countryside got – and the less houses you saw – the happier our dad seemed to be. They call the Peak District the backbone of England, and you feel like you're closer to the sky up there; closer to the *air*, even. The ground is peaty, spongy, and there are times when it's like walking about on a big pillow. Not that it's a soft, welcoming area to look at. Not up on the Dark Peak, anyway, or on Kinder Scout. The more rugged it was, the more satisfied our father was.

He looked positively serene as we stood near the edge of Kinder Downfall one day, peering down on the huge, broken rockface. It was sunny and quite hot. "Nothing like nature," he said. "Better than a film any day. Don't you think?" He was smiling at us, with the question lingering in the air, and for a moment it looked like he was going to say more, but he didn't.

Then he bought the tents.

* * *

There were two of them and quite big, too. You felt a little guilty somehow but you couldn't help thinking, "At least he does seem to have quite a lot of money. . ."

"Done this before, have you?" he challenged. We hadn't. Rockhill did that kind of thing, but we had not been there long and the chance had not come our way.

We drove out of Matlock at night, driving north-west as we had before.

"Mystery tour," he said. "For me as well as you." And he turned to grin at us where we sat in the back – a broad grin.

It was a defining moment. If you had to pick yourself a father, you'd like one who would sweep you off on an adventure but with whom you felt safe.

Travelling long distances meant nothing to him, but the time of night and the long drive soon wore down the excitement Dan and I were feeling. We fell asleep, Dan on me and me with my head on our sleeping bags. The Landrover was draughty and light fingers of warm air wandered over our faces as we dozed off.

When I woke up, the Landrover had stopped and John was not sitting behind the wheel.

I got a shock when the door beside me suddenly opened and I saw his figure in the darkness.

"We're here. Out you get," he said cheerfully.

I still felt blurry from sleep. "Where? Where's 'here'?" I asked.

"I've no idea! Which is the whole point, isn't it? We'll see in the morning."

He told us he had left the roads and tracks an hour ago and set off across the countryside with the deliberate intention of losing us all. If someone else had done it there could have been real trouble; the landscape can get too soft or too stony for cars and there are hidden holes and old lead mines and all sorts of hazards, as we knew from our previous explorations.

As for where we were exactly, my instinct was that we were high up, but that was all I could sense. There was an inner exhilaration bubbling away because I was so completely disorientated. It helped that it was a cloudy night and you couldn't see more than a few metres without some form of artificial light. Wherever we were, I had the vague suspicion that you couldn't just camp anywhere up here, but I wasn't going to argue about it.

The ground had that springy consistency and it wasn't easy to put up the tents. John left me and Dan to it with ours and we got hopelessly confused even in the bright light from the jeep's headlights, which made the surrounding darkness blacker still. John got his tent up as though he'd written the instructions himself and then helped us with ours, which was bigger. He didn't say anything but we suspected a kind of friendly contempt at our efforts. It was worth it, though, to see how perfect he made it. With its green canvas stretched taut by the guy-ropes it looked almost solid. Then he unloaded the jeep, casually giving us two brand new bicycle lamps to use in the tent for lighting.

We made the inside of the tent really cosy, talking very quietly because everything was quiet out here.

"Can I join you? Not too tired, I hope?" John was kind of shy now we were settled in our tent.

"Yes – come in," Dan said with lordly importance.

John ducked in under the outer flap and all at once the space was tiny with him in it. For a second I was angry with him.

He said, "I don't know if you're hungry, but. . ."

He had brought bottles and cans and a tin opener and a box of biscuits, all in a rucksack. My anger vanished as quickly as it had come.

"You think of everything," I joked, and he smiled back at me.

"Officer's job – to look after his troops. We'll light a fire in the morning for breakfast, but this should hold you for now."

We had cold baked beans and carrots that tasted of some strange chemical, and ginger beer. It was disgusting and we loved it. The biscuits were shortbread and I've loved shortbread ever since.

John did his watching-us-eat thing. He seemed sorry when it was over. "Well . . . I suppose that's it."

Dan said, "You'll be lonely all by yourself." He was tired and his defences were down.

John wasn't sarcastic as he sometimes could be. "I don't get lonely."

"Liar," I said sleepily.

He smiled ruefully and began to talk. "I don't know what it is. Even when I was your age, I had this feeling I was all I needed. I was happy just to potter about, doing whatever I wanted to . . . looking, listening. Selfish really."

"When you were little," I said. "No one's like that when they're little."

"Well I think I was. . . And I don't think we change that much when we get older. Sad, but true – people don't change all that much. I mean . . . you two seem to be the same two people I knew ten years ago."

"I don't remember it," Dan said. "Is that bad?"

Our father thought for a long time, squatting there on his haunches. "Look, it's not your fault, Dan. It was me. I'm not a people-person, that's what I've been saying. I've mostly been on my own. Meeting your mother – that was a kind of gift. Something extraordinary. And – perhaps – she was a gift who should have been given to someone else. Someone who could be the kind of person she needed – a people-person. But there we are. She loved me and I loved her and it was terrible when she died. Just terrible, for all of us. And then I was so restless. I couldn't see myself stuck in Manchester. I wanted to be doing things. It was . . . it was something I had to do. I told myself I could provide for you better if I got back to being the person I had been for most of my life. Now I'm thinking that was a kind of excuse and I simply wanted to be selfish again."

He looked so worried I wanted to help.

"We were OK," I said gently. He needed reassurance and it wasn't a need he was used to, so I said the words and an extraordinary thing happened, because in saying them they became true and reassuring.

In the silence that followed there was a lot of emotion washing around in that little tent. Most of it mine, I daresay.

"Well," he said, and stopped. "Well. I'm here now."

He gathered up the things he had brought and put them back in the rucksack. Before he ducked out of the tent again he pointed at the lamps and said, "Keep them on for as long as you like. I've got plenty of batteries," which was a way of letting us know he wouldn't get cross if we were scared of the dark.

Then it was like he really didn't want to leave, because after a moment he popped his head back into the tent and cleared his throat before he spoke. "We'll get the bikes to go with them. Soon. Goodnight."

Dan and I lay there and we should have been talking away but we didn't need to say a single thing. There we were in the middle of nowhere and all at once we felt warm and safe and something else as well. There was that tiny sensation running along up high in your consciousness, almost not a part of you: a pure thread of happiness.

In the morning we saw the house.

Lowlake.

2

Saturated by sunlight, the tent was a magical green when I woke up. It took me a moment to see that the bicycle lamps were still on. Dan was asleep, his hair standing on end and his jaw slack. I remembered the feeling of happiness of last night as I looked at him. Asleep he was ever so vulnerable and my heart went out to him. To protect the moment, I let him sleep on. When he was awake it wasn't so easy to get those tender feelings.

So I got dressed quietly, with some difficulty because the roof of the tent was low, and brushed my hair.

Somewhere outside a curlew was calling. We had seen several up here, dainty-stepping drab birds with impossibly long, drooping beaks. The call was a thin, sad note which could have been made by a badly-constructed wooden whistle. Closer to the tent, there was a faint crackling noise.

Outside John was bending over the flames of a fire. He had gathered stones to surround it and I saw he had brought ready-made kindling with him to make things simpler. The neat strips of wood were a little green and there was a lot of smoke.

Through it I could see the house: Lowlake.

It wavered in the heat from the fire, as in a vision. It was a long low building set in a wide scoop of open land beneath us, about five hundred metres away. Built of grey stone, it had small windows even on the ground floor, indicating that there was a lot of weather round here that needed keeping out. There was one other proper floor above the ground floor and then, in the crumbling stone-tiled roof, there were these little pointy dormer windows.

Even on a bright morning it was not an agreeable building. The best it could offer was a stubborn, settled look: "There's no shifting *me*." You could see low walls to the back of the house and within them the abandoned garden grew tall and wild.

It was as though John had heard me looking at the house, because he turned and smiled. "I didn't do much of a job getting us away from civilization, did I? I had no idea we were right by that."

"I wouldn't call it civilization, exactly," I said.

We sat staring at the house while we ate breakfast. Dan was more interested in how much sizzling sausage-grease he could get on his face, but John and I kept looking at it. He wondered aloud what it was, whether it was derelict, what its history had been.

I was pleased he was talking to us now just like an ordinary, easy-going person, and I joined in. "Well, there's no one there now."

He said, "Oh, up round here I'd think people might go on living in a house even if it was falling down."

"You mean they're looking at us now?"

He waved a sausage at the house. "Green with envy, they are. Haven't seen a sausage in years."

"There isn't anyone there. It's empty."

"Well – let's take a look, shall we? When we've cleaned up here. Though I think it's Dan who's going to need most of the cleaning."

Dan beamed and so did I. Like the slightly irresponsible mystery-tour thing, the idea of snooping around the old house brought us all closer together.

It was obvious and yet still surprising: the nearer you got to the house the bigger it seemed. There was no evidence that there had ever been a lawn at the front; the ground there was strangely lumpy, sprinkled with tufts of tall grasses. John stopped for a moment to take Dan by surprise and whirl him around, giving him an "aeroplane", even though he was a little too old and a little too big for that now.

I guessed it was the first time in his life John had ever done such a thing, and I was still smiling at Dan's breathless laughter when I left them to it and went on towards the house.

The world jolted: I lurched to one side and sank into the ground up to my hip. It was as wet here as though the land was floating on an inland sea. I was so shocked I didn't think of the danger immediately; I was mostly mad that my clothes were soaked through, because I didn't have a change with me.

John's voice came from behind me. "Don't move a muscle, Amanda. Stay just like you are." It was so calm and clear that then I was worried – really worried.

I heard him coming. I was slipping deeper, still going to one side. My shoulder submerged.

"Don't look round. Stretch your hand back to me."

Shoulder muscles straining, I reached my free hand back towards him as far as I could. He took hold of my wrist in a grasp so strong it was painful. His other hand came into the water to get a grip on my shirt, winding it round to get a good purchase on it. And he pulled. Gradually I was eased out, till I could look round and see him crouched on firm ground, pulling away. And then I could give him my other arm and it was easy for him to wrench me up to a standing position.

Dan had a look of alarm fixed on his face, which now relaxed as he gave way to helpless sniggering. John said, not unkindly, "Shut up Dan, it's not funny." He was still looking at me, though. "Amanda, I'm sorry. It was my fault."

"I don't think so," I said loyally.

"Let's get you to the car, shall we?"

"I don't want it to spoil our day."

"I think we should get back to the hotel, anyway. We've had our fun."

Dan made a noise somehow expressing both discontent and annoyance with me for putting an end to the fun. I wanted the day to go on, too, so I kept John talking, asking him questions, trying to get him cheerful again, while the sun did its job and began to dry me.

We agreed how weird it was, this hidden water. It wasn't a bog and nothing like quicksand (John said). Just a natural phenomenon. Water does appear in the strangest places. He cited some natural spring on Mount Isa, in Northern Queensland, and I got him talking about Australia too. He was enthusiastic then and admitted how hard it had been for him to leave, because the country had got a real hold on him.

"But that's dwindling now," he said, and his eyes twinkled.

Now we're back where we were before my water-accident, I thought. So I said cajolingly, "Let's have a look at the house – like we said we would. There can't be water all the way round."

He hesitated then, but I persuaded him. We could now see the limits of the watery bit – it was confined to the tufty, lumpy area of land. He was the one who established this, and after that you could see his sense of enterprise returning.

I said, "Oh, come on. Do let's have a look round. Now we've got this far."

He held up his hands in surrender. "All right, then – you win. Now let's all shut up and get trespassing!"

So, in a way, it was all my fault, because if I hadn't talked him round we'd have turned our backs on Lowlake and none of the horrible things would have happened.

We went all the way round the house, looking for a way in. The less possible it seemed, the more you wanted it. Isn't that always the way? We tried the big front door and the one at the back, but of course they were locked. It was so frustrating, pressing one's face up against some cobwebby window and being able to see little or nothing of what was inside. All of the windows were tightly-closed. Some of those on the ground floor were shuttered on the inside so you looked at blank wood. These were at the far end of the house.

One thing at least was clear, no one was going to

start shouting at us: if ever a house was deserted, it was this one.

"I really don't want to break anything to get in. It's not the end of the world if we don't," John said at last. He was beginning to feel the embarrassment of the adult embarked on a childish escapade which isn't working out.

But Dan's criminal tendencies had by now been aroused to a high pitch. "We'll get in all right!" he called shrilly, tugging and pushing at windows we'd already proved wouldn't open.

"No. Come on, let's go and find somewhere to eat lunch. Food, Dan – how about it?"

"Not yet," came the call.

"Oh, do come on."

"This one's coming! It's coming!"

He was by one of two small windows on either side of the front door, set up at around the height of his head. Really, there wasn't any way he could get more leverage on the window than I had a few minutes ago.

But the fact remained, it had now squeezed itself open a little way.

"Well. . ." John said reluctantly.

"Come on – I've done it!"

John went over and quite easily pulled the window back until it was fully open. "All right. All right. In you hop. I'll give you a leg up."

Now Dan wasn't so sure. "You go first."

"I'd never fit through there."

"Well, you, then, Mandy."

"Oh, thanks a lot," I said, but I didn't mind.

"You're still a bit wet," Dan said helpfully. "You'll slide in quite easy."

John made a stirrup with his hands and I was propelled up to the little window and then tipped through it like a torpedo in its tube. I got into a right tangle, because I was going in head-first. I hesitated, balancing with my waist on the window-sill. All I could do was to inch forward and downward with my hands reaching for the floor. I fell the last couple of feet and landed on stone tiling. This time when I heard Dan laughing I was cross. I shouted, "You should have done it, Shorty – only you were too scared!"

My voice echoed, crashing around the house like a rude, violent intruder, and then I was scared myself. But of course there was nobody one could wake up here, by yelling like that.

Unless you counted whatever that was – scurrying away in the darkness. . . A mouse? And I bet myself there were bats here, and I bet myself I didn't like bats, though I had never actually seen one. Weren't there stories about them getting tangled in your hair?

I was standing in a wide hallway. There were doors on either side of me and in the middle of the hall I could make out that a corridor ran both ways.

Smack in the centre of everything a great big staircase led upwards into darkness. The house had grown in size as we neared it: now it loomed over me.

As silence returned after my bawling out to the others, I felt the building's quiet embrace and within the space of a second I felt oddly at home – it was like I was being welcomed. The house hadn't given up hope at all, I felt; it was solid, patient, waiting for occupants or visitors like us. *It's rather nice*, I found myself thinking.

"Everything all right?" John's face was in the little window by the door.

"Oh yes."

"Can you get us in?"

"I don't know. . . Um – oh, yes – yes, I think I can."

Beside the door, placed with perfect convenience, a bunch of dark keys hung on a hook. It was obvious that the biggest key opened the front door, but first I had bolts to draw back.

Light flooded into the hallway, revealing my footprints on the dusty flagstones.

John and Dan stepped in eagerly.

Something small and black swept out through the doorway in ragged, super-fast flight. A real-life bat. Dan ducked with a short scream – and I laughed nervously. The laughter echoed for a little while after I had finished.

*   *   *

With John being very grown-up and reminding us to be careful at every step, we explored. The excitement faded pretty quickly. However many rooms a house has, and Lowlake had a lot, there's not much to maintain suspense when there's nothing whatever in them. So there was only the darkness to entertain us and Dan and me soon got bored.

The room with the shutters at the end of the house was the one John liked best. It was panelled with some light-coloured wood – the same wood the shutters were made of – and here there were bookshelves to relieve the monotony of bare plastered walls.

"Isn't it good?" he said lightly. He managed to open one of the shutters and we looked out at the raw, rolling countryside.

"See, I don't know about you city folk, but this is what I like to see when I look out of a window."

"You mean – nothing at all?" Dan said scornfully.

"I mean something big and unspoilt."

"Yeah – like I said – nothing at all," said Dan.

"I think I've been ruined for city life. Coming from Australia."

And John sighed. I was standing slightly behind him and it seemed it had to have been him.

One of us sighed, anyway.

Or, to put it another way, there was a sigh. . .

3

We looked around upstairs too of course, and of course it was all empty there as well. But John was quietly appreciative of the house and now it was as if it was welcoming him and not me, because I was beginning to get the slightest bit twitchy about it, although I couldn't explain why. At the time I put it down to the presence of the bats. A couple more had whizzed by us unexpectedly.

"A very sound house, by and large," John commented pompously. "But I imagine the roof isn't all it should be – that's how the bats get in, I'd guess."

We were on the top floor, where the ceilings were lower and the windows stuck out. He went on, "Cosy, isn't it, up here?"

Cosy? A very sound house perhaps, but hardly cosy.

"I'm hungry," Dan finally said, as he was bound to.

So we left. I had to leave last through the little window, after locking the door, and it wasn't easy.

John was very quiet as we skirted the watery grass and went back up to our campsite. While we packed up the tents he glanced down at the house every now and then.

"Shame you didn't get us into the middle of nowhere after all," I said cheerfully.

"Oh well – close enough!" he smiled back.

"When's *lunch*?" Dan called peevishly.

John drove us away using the dirt-and-stone track which led up to the house. He was interested to see where the track went. It led us up out of the shallow depression and gradually downwards across wild country. About a mile on, it joined a proper road.

As John came to the crossroads I saw the sign.

"Wait," I said, and scrambled out to have a look.

Sagging down, it was a white wooden sign with a pointed end which faced the direction we had come from. The stake holding it up had rotted through and broke off in my hand when I tried to straighten it. John got out of the car to see it too.

" 'LOWLAKE' " he read aloud. "Well well. Shame we didn't see this before – then we might have guessed there was water waiting for us. Though I doubt it. You don't get much higher above sea level than we were up there. 'Lowlake.' Presumably the name of the house. Well – let's put it back on the map, shall we?"

And, despite Dan's piteous cries for sustenance ("Crisps – anything – I don't mind"), John spent a little time driving what was left of the staked sign back into the ground.

Then we drove on, coming soon to Essop, the local village, where the dwellings had the same stone-tiled roofs that Lowlake had.

John bought us lunch and drinks in a pub – and he took a long time about it too. He wanted a long talk with the landlord, and I'm sure the subject of their conversation was Lowlake.

But he didn't say any more about the house to us. After a week in each other's company we were all tuning in to each other and he had got the message that we were fed up with it.

When next we heard about Lowlake it was in a letter from John. We were back at Rockhill, grinding out the last of the summer term.

The letter said he had bought Lowlake: it was our new home.

"*Surprise!*" he wrote, and he could just as well have put "*Shock!*" because that was what we got when we read the news.

At Rockhill mail was distributed during tea and we were in the building which served as a dining hall. It had a corrugated-iron roof and was very noisy when it rained. Around us one hundred boys and girls wearing track-suit bottoms and T-shirts munched on starch and and drank deep brown tea to the accompaniment of a continuous rattle of cutlery.

Too much talking was frowned upon at mealtimes and we spoke quietly.

"I don't believe it," Dan moaned. "What are we going to do there?"

"We'll be getting bikes," I reminded him, though I was feeling funny about it too. "New ones. You won't have to ride my old wreck any more."

"We'll need them. You've got to go miles before you even see a sheep up there."

When you're the oldest you find yourself saying things which sound sensible and responsible but which you don't believe in particularly, so while I murmured on about how it might be really good fun living at Lowlake with John, all the while I felt this dull hopelessness. We weren't meant to be stuck out in the country. We belonged in the bustle of the city when we weren't at school. John wanted to live miles from nowhere because it suited him; he hadn't consulted us at all.

We read the letter again, sitting side by side at the trestle table.

"...*I couldn't resist it! It's going to be a lot of work to get it up and running as a family house, but I'm here right now, writing this in the library — at* <u>night</u>*, because we already have the electricity connected! During the day the place is full of workmen and I potter around at all hours with a paint-brush myself. (I told you I like to potter.) By the time you get here your rooms, at least, will be ready, and even the roof may be finished. The kitchen will be in working order too, if a little rough-and-ready. I've discovered that the house is 17th century in origin and was once used as a convalescent home. But to me it says 'family home' — just marvellous for children — and I think you'll agree — when we've got it finished of course.*"

The letter rambled on as John enthused more about Lowlake and what was happening with it and what rapid progress he had made already.

"He's insane," Dan said.

"Who is?" said Brian, the ginger-haired boy on my right. He had a look of disgust on his face, having just discovered that the piece of bread he was buttering had been buttered on the other side by a previous owner.

"Our father."

" 'Who Art In Heaven' ," Brian smirked wittily. "What about him?"

"He's bought a new house," I said gloomily.

"Not new," Dan corrected, "Old. And horrible."

"Well at least you've got a house to go to," Brian said, hiding the twice-buttered delicacy under the communal stack of sliced bread in the middle of the table. "I've got to go to Malaysia for the holidays," he said gloomily.

"Oh yeah – terrible for you," I said.

"It'll be all right, I suppose. But it's not a home. You're lucky."

One evening in late July we drove to Lowlake once again. Our new home. The sky was red and empty and John was as bright as could be. For a man of few words he was babbling.

"The only way to bring up children. . . Fresh air all the day long. . . A feeling of freedom and space. . . You're going to love it. . . Really, it's the perfect place for us."

Possibly he was aware how we felt about living in the wilds of the Peak District and was trying to overcome our dislike of the idea, but his enthusiasm and sincerity were so huge that you were even more put off.

Our silence only prompted him to talk more – having to speak loudly because the Landrover was so noisy.

"I've been thinking about schools, too. Rockhill was only a temporary measure, after all. But you two quite like boarding school now, don't you? As a way of life and learning and so on?"

"I don't know!" Dan shouted from the back. "We didn't have a choice, did we?"

"I think we'd like to stay together, anyway," I said.

"Well. . ." John tried to keep the irritation out of his voice. "It might not work like that. Most proper boarding schools tend to be single sex."

"There's all sorts of schools in Manchester," I offered tentatively. Here we were, going to a new home we didn't want to go to and when the holidays were over we were to be packed off to separate schools. Life seemed as threatening as the sky.

"Look – forget about Manchester. A day school isn't possible – it'd be a heck of a drive. I can't look after you day-to-day – I mean – I just can't."

We came to the top of the world and looked down. The little windows of Lowlake looked up at us blankly from the shallow basin below.

There was a man working on the roof. He was a thacker, a craftsman who works with stone tiles. A van and a small car were parked at the side of the house and around the watery danger in front of it John had put up a low wire fence.

The van was the thacker's and the little car belonged to Mrs Martindale, who came twice a week to help with the cleaning. She was about to go now, which was why the car was here. Her husband, a small man with a moustache, drove her to Lowlake and then came to pick her up when she was finished. We were to find he was very protective of her, although why he should be was a mystery since she was much larger than he was and more capable in every way.

It was Mrs Martindale who showed us to our rooms, with the grim satisfaction of a jailor.

"Oh it's a fair place to stop, round Essop way," she said dourly as we dragged our suitcases up the stairs behind her. "Very popular with the tourists."

With this she managed to convey that this part of the country was not fit for making a home in.

However, Lowlake was habitable by now in a spartan sort of way. Our rooms were ready for us. They faced each other across the first floor corridor and in each was, simply, a bed, a wardrobe and chest of drawers. There were bedside lights on little tables and narrow rugs to step on when you put your feet out of bed. The rugs were brightly striped and new; the furniture was lacquered pine: when it came to home furnishings, our father was not imaginative. His own bedroom was a long way down the corridor.

It was like arriving at some kind of depressing hotel – one which was going out of business. The other rooms on this floor, and there were several of them, were stark and empty. I noticed for the first time how heavy the doors were here, and how every one of them had a business-like lock set into it.

Mrs Martindale left us with, "There's sandwiches in the kitchen when you want to come down and get them. I don't cook, you understand, but it's your first day here and all."

We were in Dan's room. The floorboards were dark and polished and had an institutional look.

"Well," Dan said, trying to be cheerful about it, "Here we are."

"Yes. Here we are."

We didn't meet the thacker that day. He and the Martindales had spirited themselves away by the time we had unpacked and come down again.

We had checked out the bathroom – definite hairy spider territory. The old linoleum on the floor was cracked in places and the new bathroom suite looked much too small for the size of the room. So far there was just the one spider exploring the sink. You always get more insects in the country.

But at least there were no more bats. John assured us of that as we ate some rather dull sandwiches in the kitchen, where the only decoration was a calendar hung on a wall. "The funny thing is," he said, "none of the workmen found any sign of bats being here in the first place. The ones we saw must have been strays, I suppose."

He was as animated as he had been on the drive here. We would all be going together to look for more furnishings. So far we only had the basics, he knew – he wanted us to help choose stuff for Lowlake. It was our home now.

At one moment I caught him looking a little desperate and I couldn't help feeling sympathetic. He was doing his best – what more could he do? And, surely, wherever we had started our new lives with our father, it would have seemed this strange.

The worst blow of all was when we discovered that, no matter what you did with the aerial, TV reception was hopeless. Siberian snowstorm on every channel. Then we learned that John didn't care because he had an old-fashioned attitude about making one's own amusements. And in any case, as he pointed out, there was a big radio in here, and we had a few video tapes and Dan had his Playstation.

"And, er, while we're making our own amusements, what will you be doing?" Dan asked with dangerous politeness.

"I'm going to write a book!" John said, with modest embarrassment.

"Oh."

"I've had quite an interesting life. I thought I'd have a go at the old memoirs. Even if it never got published I'd still get something out of it. It would be a way of . . . putting my life into perspective. Good idea, don't you think?"

"Yes. Good idea," I said dully.

"But don't worry – I'll have plenty of time for you. We'll do lots. And maybe we'll get satellite TV sometime – that'd work. Oh, and look – look. . ."

He jumped up from his high-backed Windsor chair and led the way into the old scullery, which was just off the kitchen on the way to the back door. In the scullery, leaning against the washing machine, stood three brand-new mountain bikes with enough gears to get you to the top of Everest.

Dan and I exchanged glances of delight and all three of us beamed at each other. What our father said he would do, he did do. We'd be all right here, eventually.

We went to bed quite late, after watching one of our videos, the worst of them: about a serial killer. The tape was Dan's of course. I think he watched it again and again to try and desensitize himself to horror films, but it got to him every time. Looking at John's disapproving face I thought to myself, *Oh well done, Dan. Bang go the satellite channels.* Though I have to say I never like it either, when the camera lurks just behind some actor's shoulder as he tiptoes through some dangerous place that no one with any sense would have gone into in the first place.

The video could have been why Dan came into my room just when I was settling down under the covers. I was ever so tired.

"What's the matter?" I asked.

"Can I get in with you?"

"No you can't. You're too old."

He didn't go on about it. He sat on the end of the bed and said in a low voice, "It feels so odd, being here."

"Well, that's because it is odd."

"I don't like it."

"We didn't like Rockhill when we went there – but it was OK after a bit."

"I know. And he's nice, isn't he. I really do like him."

"Me too. When he's not being too politically correct."

"I wish there wasn't just him, though. Know what I mean?"

"Mmn," I said. Dan must have been thinking about our mother. She had got leukaemia and died so long ago that he was thinking about her as a kind of theory, not as a person who had actually lived. That was how I thought of her, anyway, when I did think about her, and he was that little bit younger so it must have been like that for him too.

As usual I tried to say the right thing. "We've got each other."

Trite, but it worked. He nodded solemnly and sat there for a second longer before he got up and padded back to his room.

John was quite crazy sometimes. . . While I lay there he was doing some decorating in the hall. . . Crazy. And I did rather want him to come upstairs soon, so we were all on the same floor, even if we were in different rooms.

I was dozing off. With the light on – just for tonight. . .

The footsteps, when I heard them, came not from below, but above. Light footsteps, running. Then pausing. Running on.

There was no one upstairs. None of the rooms up there was going to be used.

I sat up in bed to listen better.

No – now there was no sound at all, anywhere in the house. It was – must have been – something to do with that video. Something from my own imagination. I had been on the edge of sleep and it was a kind of dream.

Only I knew it hadn't been.

4

The morning was as bright as Texas. It was unbelievable how different the house felt. The sunshine poured optimism into me and warmed away the fears of last night. It couldn't have been footsteps I heard ... that is, if I had indeed heard anything at all. And if I had, might it not have been a rogue bat? Or, mice – with an echo – maybe. Those upper rooms probably did have an echo. And oh, what a fabulous day it was!

But at the back of my mind I still had a little fragment of doubt. I wouldn't tell Dan, though. He was anti-Lowlake enough already.

We didn't spend a happier day in all our time at Lowlake. Dan started the day in a cheerful frame of mind too and John was delighted. After breakfast he swept us off on a bike ride, speeding along on the top of the world.

We zoomed down to Essop and found a bookshop there. It was run by Mr Burton, a tweedy old gent with what appeared to be tobacco-stained white hair, and orange ends to the fingers he held his cigarettes in. He had a real smoker's voice as well, a bubbling kind of growl, but he seemed friendly in a detached sort of way.

Some of his stock was new and naturally there was a lot of touristy stuff, but mostly he dealt in second-hand books.

"Choose," said John simply.

Our hands were dusty by the time we finished in the shop and there was a stack of books on Mr Burton's counter, waiting to be picked up by John at a later time.

I was into historical novels round about then, so that was what I picked out. Dan helped himself to several interactive adventure books that were more comics than anything else, and John bought him one very big, very second-hand copy of a book he couldn't resist because it was so unusual. "A real collector's item, this," he said. Dan's face said that if he himself wanted to start some sort of collection this type of thing would be low on his list. The book's cover was extremely colourful in its faded way and it was called *One Hundred and One Wonders for Boys*. Written in the 1930s, it was a collection of odd facts and things to do on a wet day.

But today it was sunny, and we were off again, cycling in convoy to the bigger town of Stindale. This was a whole ten miles further on, but we wished it could have been further still – we were having such fun.

"Um, what are we doing here?" Dan asked breathlessly as we pedalled up the steep High Street. "Lunch?"

"Lunch – shopping – everything!" John shouted back.

You needed your lowest gear on that hill. I had never had a bike with so many gears before and had been continually changing them just for the joy of it, but not here.

We left our bikes at the war memorial and "did the town" thoroughly. Everything we did, we did at speed and with quite fantastic relish. What we did most was shop. That was another first for me: a huge shopping binge. Once you've bought more than, say, five things, and you know you're going on to get more, you get caught up in a happy hysteria. Euphoria, that's the word. What made it best of all was that we didn't have to carry anything once we'd bought it. It was like being a millionaire – Dan and me would just hang about while John made arrangements either to pick up whatever it was we had selected or for it to be delivered.

What we were buying was things for the house. We started off in an old auction house which had been converted into a second-hand shop. It was big and crammed with articles which were mostly old and unwanted with good reason, though quite a few were genuine antiques with prices to match.

We looked for stuff that would especially suit Lowlake, which was, after all, an old house. There were all sorts of oddities to look at apart from the furniture, such as old clothes – some even from Victorian times – and medals and clocks and silverware and really just about everything you could think of. As John said, it was an Aladdin's cave. After an hour in there we went to other shops, where John paid for sofas, carpets, curtains, table lamps. . . And all the time he took our advice – actually consulted us on decisions which adults usually made all by themselves!

"I think the blue is better," Dan would say, and John would nod seriously and say, "You're right."

Once – trying to remember what it was like to be responsible – I suggested, "Couldn't we get these things cheaper in Manchester or Derby – in a shopping mall?"

John grinned. He leaned down and whispered, "We are keeping in with the natives. We support our local tradesmen and they get to know us and like us." His grin widened. "And besides – it's fun, isn't it?"

It certainly was.

*　　*　　*

After a massive lunch in the biggest of the two hotels in Stindale things got even better.

John took us back to the electrical shop where we had ordered the table lamps. He bought us a state-of-the-art micro sound sytem with a mini disc player and a set of headphones I picked out to go with it.

"For the nursery," he said. "Sorry – it was the nursery, but now we'll call it your sitting room."

That was the first we had heard of having our own private room for reading and relaxation. It was situated right by our bedrooms, with one of the best views in the house.

Dan was astonished when John put up no fight at all about getting a hand-held games console with a colour screen – one he had been lusting after for months. In fact, John apologized that we wouldn't be getting our own personal computers till later in the year: he had a contact in electronics in the far East and he was going to do some kind of deal when the bloke came over. If the portable John used for his own work was the sort of gear we could look forward to getting, I was prepared to wait for something that good.

If we had a mini-disc-player and a games console we must have mini-discs too and games too. . . For the first time that day I wished we were taking our purchases home now. I said it. I said, "I can't wait to get these home."

He was either clever or lucky. By involving us so thoroughly in all this he had made us think of Lowlake as "home".

During the next few days Dan and I were caught up in our father's obsession to get the house finished. He collected some of the stuff we'd bought and other things were delivered and we worked away like mad, organizing the main rooms of the house. There was the big reception room, the dining room and our sitting room upstairs to do, and the halls had to be decked out with stuff too, so they didn't look so empty.

John wouldn't let us help him with "his" room, the library, and we didn't let him interfere with our sitting room.

One little reception room we hardly touched at all. It was near the front door, small and dark and extremely damp. "Get round to that one later," John remarked. "Much later. It'll do for coats and umbrellas and things."

The main reception rooms had these odd brass instruments on the walls, fitted in Victorian days. They were speaking tubes for the masters of the house to talk to their servants in the kitchen. John had burnished the old things till they shone and we had self-important fun talking to each other on them as we worked.

"Could you bring that chest into the dining

room? It'd go quite well under the window now we've moved the sideboard. . ."

Of course you did have to shout a little, since the tubes were not as effective as they had been when new, so now you could hear the voice of the person you were talking to coming from down the hall as well as through the tube.

John had played safe when it came to the pictures we hung in the rooms and halls. The ones in the second-hand shop had been stained and dirty, and he had only bought one there: a monochrome print of an early steam ship ploughing through a heavy sea. We ended up with a lot more sea scenes in fake-old frames, in which tea-clippers raced along with all sails set; or smoke billowed across naval battles of the Napoleonic Wars. The other pictures were copies of famous landscapes which had been painted in the 1800s; great craggy places with noble deer sniffing the air under thunderous skies.

As John said, doubtfully, after we'd hung them and re-hung them in every possible position and combination, "Well, they'll do, anyway."

When you walked around the house these bargain reproductions gave you the sensation that you were in some kind of public building. You can't buy a houseful of pictures all in one go and not get this institutional effect.

But our room was just great. We had film posters on the walls there, and a huge map of the world. I played my few mini-discs to death. The richness of sound you got from that system – you wouldn't believe it.

And Dan played his games console. I began to wish he'd get tired of it and go back to the Playstation: the sounds this thing made were like someone plucking at the teeth of a comb. On and on. Plinky plonky. Talk about an irritating and intrusive noise. Though I always had the option of wearing my headphones, something stopped me: the feeling that if someone came into the room I wouldn't know they were there.

What with plinky plonky and my super-bass sounds and all the house-arranging activity, Lowlake was a frenetic and cheerful place for a day or two. There wasn't a moment to be gloomy or worried about anything.

There comes the point when you're sitting down resting and you think, *Well, better get up – better get on with it, I suppose*, and then you realize that there's nothing much left to do so you might as well stay where you are. We were in our private sitting room and, to my relief, Dan had just turned off the plinky plonk machine.

The house went quiet.

John was in his room. He was still busy, even if we'd had enough. That morning he had taken out the old one and put a working lock on the library door. I thought it was odd at the time, but he had been so carried away by all the arranging and refurbishing that maybe he just couldn't stop. Odd, though, all the same.

Dan was reading his big book of *Wonders*. Flicking through it, anyway.

"Mandy. . ." he said casually.

"Mmn. What?"

"Have you been getting up at night?"

"What do you mean?"

"Have you been wandering around, I mean."

"No. Why?"

"Sometimes I can hear someone."

"Could be John," I said cautiously. "He never seems to sleep."

"He's downstairs all the time. This was up above."

Dan was very rigid sitting there and I knew he was frightened. I had to be honest and at the same time I mustn't encourage his fear.

"Well . . . I have heard things. Not footsteps – they'd be much heavier. I think there might be some little animal up there. Or even birds. Maybe a bat or two. That's what it is. I did hear something, though, the first night we were here."

"I hear it every night. And I think I can hear whispering."

"Oh, no, I don't think so."

I got up and went to sit on the arm of his chair, so I could put my arm round him. Dan used to get nightmares when he was little: we didn't want all that starting up again.

"What are we doing today?" I asked brightly.

"Nothing," he said glumly. "John hasn't got any suggestions. I asked him."

"He'll do things with us when he's stopped running around like a chicken with its head cut off. When everything's finished."

"Well, what are we going to do?"

"I think what we ought to do," I said firmly, "is go upstairs and investigate. Then we'll know there's nothing to worry about."

Dan took some persuading, which was unlike him when there was adventure in prospect, but I was convinced that this was the way to lay his fears to rest – and mine too.

The top floor was as it had been when we first broke into Lowlake – deserted. We walked up and down it, with Dan sticking close to my side. The rooms were empty and characterless. I was reminded that this really was an enormous house for just three people and I had to wonder what we were doing, living here. . .

"Hello? Hello?" My voice did have a slight echo.

We had worked out which rooms were above ours and were standing in the one over Dan's.

"Hello?" I said, louder, and joked, "Anyone there?"

Dan said, "Don't, Mandy. It's not funny."

"It does echo, though. Something small might make a noise and it could sound quite loud underneath."

"Maybe. . ."

"Not convinced?"

"I don't know," he said uneasily. "Well – perhaps. I just don't know any more."

"All right," I said coolly. "We'll keep looking. We might find a nest or something."

"If it's rats, I'd rather not."

"Don't be silly. Come on."

We looked in the last two rooms. In the last one there was a hatch in the wall. It was bolted and the bolt was stiff.

"What are you doing?" Dan asked.

"What's it look like? There's a loft up above and this must be the way to it."

"Oh."

"Go and get the lamps off the bikes."

The idea of searching by torchlight was irresistible to Dan. By the time he got back I was through the hatch and peering up into the gloom, standing on the steep, ladder-type of stairs which led up and to the side. The torches weren't absolutely essential because there were still some tiny gaps in the roof and light filtered through.

We went up.

The loft was good. It ran the length of the house,

very low. You bent double to move around it and there were still beams you had to avoid in case you bumped your head, and wooden joists you had to tread on so you didn't go through the plaster between them.

There were two big water tanks up there. One was connected and obviously newer, being made of metal. The other was filthy and wooden-sided. I banged it with my hand and it echoed.

"See? There could be something in here. Some animal. And if there was, it'd make a lot of noise."

"No. It wouldn't sound like what I heard."

"We won't know till we've looked," I said.

There was a wooden lid to shift and it was heavy and awkward. The lining of the tank was of a dull metal, probably lead, which might have been why the tank had been taken out of use.

There were no animals inside and no trace of them. There was, however, a traveller's trunk made of wood, with leather straps around it.

"Hey." I said. "Now what about that?"

Dan peered in, using his lamp. "That wouldn't make a noise."

"No – I mean let's have a look."

"Oh – yes."

Before we could do anything about getting into the tank and getting the trunk out, there was a great scraping noise near our heads. Dan jumped a mile.

"What's that?"

It was a thoroughly practical-sounding noise, as we realized after the first shock, and we went downstairs to take a look.

What we saw when we got outside was that the Landrover was gone and the thacker's van was here. I was piqued that John hadn't taken us with him: a Dad who knew his stuff would have asked if we wanted to trail along, however boring the expedition he was making. There was a fine mist around the house; a phenomenon that happened more usually in the early morning, and a product of the house being situated in a dip with water in it, I supposed.

The thacker was on the roof with a bucket of stone tiles. The noise we had heard was him getting his long wooden ladder into place. We knew his name was Mr Davies because John was always wondering aloud when he would get back to finish the job.

He stared down at us silently, a strangely elongated man with huge hands, who looked well over sixty and was thoroughly crabby. John had said, "These skilled craftsmen – think they're royalty or something!"

While we watched, Mr Davies' boot suddenly slipped and his leg straightened involuntarily, dislodging a big stone slate which shot down towards us almost as if it had been aimed.

Dan jumped one way and I jumped the other and

the tile shattered loudly on the path. Splinters of stone shot about like shrapnel and we were lucky we weren't hit.

Dan recovered his composure quicker than I did – and I saw him running to Mr Davies' ladder. It was leaning to one side, for on the roof Mr Davies had tumbled down to the gutter and hung there by his fingertips, unable to move an inch, since the old guttering was already bending and breaking as he dangled there.

I saw what Dan was trying to do and I joined him at the foot of the ladder. It seemed Mr Davies had kicked it away as he fell. Together we worked it back to a position right by Mr Davies.

He got a boot on it . . . a hand . . . and then the gutter was relieved of his weight and he could manoeuvre himself so he was off the roof and on to the ladder. No one had shouted or screamed or made any kind of noise during the whole drama. Now Mr Davies breathed out so loudly we could hear it.

He said, "Thanks."

5

"More tea, Mr Davies?"

"It wouldn't be wasted. Thank you."

We were in the kitchen and I was "mother" with the tea, acting the formal hostess in a way which made me giggle inside.

In his own fashion Mr Davies had been grateful for our help. He was at least prepared to open his mouth and talk to us, which was apparently a great privilege.

Dan said, "Do you know where John – where our father went?"

"Said he had some things to get."

"But he didn't say when he'd be back?"

"No."

"Biscuit?" I enquired lightly.

"That'd be very welcome."

He munched slowly through a digestive. "Got to get back to work soon. Be finished today. Hard to match the stone, you see, or I'd have been done long since."

"Aren't you worried about slipping again?" Dan asked.

"This place ain't going to have me," Mr Davies said mysteriously.

"What do you mean?" I wasn't the elegant hostess any more, but openly curious.

He ate some more biscuit, using the action to buy himself thinking time. Then all he said was, "Nasty old roof that. Nearly had me a couple of times."

I asked him, "We were wondering why somewhere as high up as this was called Lowlake. Was it a joke or something?"

"Joke? No. Round here, 'low' means 'high', see?"

"Why?"

"Ah – well. Goes back. I don't know when it would be, but 'low' was a word for a burial mound – or burial hill, way back in ancient times. So it's something that sticks up, and – well – it's high enough round here, so someone said this is the 'High Lake' and so they called it Lowlake. You see? Well – obviously."

"It seems weird having a lake here at all," Dan said. "Mandy fell into it when we first came."

"Did she now? Wouldn't be the first." Mr Davies

had a small smile on his face. You have to say we hadn't rescued the most agreeable man in the world.

"But it isn't a lake – it's more of a bog," I said.

"Was a lake once. They tried to fill it in, but up the water came. They've tried all sorts with this house, but you don't change it."

"Excuse me," I said carefully, "But the way you say things, it sounds like Lowlake isn't a very nice place."

"'Nice'? Haven't heard anyone use that word about it."

"But why? What's wrong with it?"

"Couldn't tell you. But you get somewhere used for what this was, well, it puts people off it. That's one thing, maybe. There's not many like me, who'll come up here to do a job or two."

"It was a convalescent home, wasn't it? What's wrong with that?"

"Who told you that?"

"Our father."

"Well. . ." Mr Davis fingered his tea cup, considering how to continue. "He'd have got a good price on this – that would be the reason to buy it. I'm careful with money myself. But I'd have been more straight with you than he was. Only fair, when all's said and done."

"We've no idea what you're talking about."

He started smiling again. "Best to be fair. You

been a help to me, only fair I should help you, if that's what you want."

"We would like to know about Lowlake." Dan said determinedly.

"Would you now. Well. . . Had a good few owners, this house, but it's best known for. . ."

"Oh do get on with it!" I said impatiently. Mr Davies, being fair or otherwise, was enjoying this far too much for my liking.

"It was a lunatic asylum," he said.

We were waiting for John. And had been all afternoon. Mr Davies had finished his work and driven off.

We had the radio on in the kitchen, tuned to a channel which was mostly music. There's something reassuring about a kitchen, a place which is practical, down-to-earth.

Our father had not phoned and now it was getting dark and quite a wind had got up outside.

Dan said, "I'm going to get another book. Back in a minute."

He went out of the room. We had not talked much, and I thought that it was quite brave of Dan, given what we now knew about our home, to go off by himself. I started to make some sandwiches – not because I didn't expect John to turn up soon, but for something to do.

There was a sound coming from the speaking

tube on the wall, I thought. It was hard to tell; the radio was playing a slow soul number, all breathy and romantic.

The speaking tube had this bell-shaped end which you either talked into or listened through. I went to pick it up.

At first I didn't hear anything except the music from the radio, and then the noise came again down the tube . . . a steady breathing sound, like someone with a bad chest. I thought, *It's the wind outside. Maybe when it's windy outside it gets into this.*

The song on the radio murmered about love and the breathing stopped in the speaking tube. And then came a whispery laugh. A kind of giggle without using vocal chords.

I put the bell-thing to my mouth. "Dan – I know it's you and it's not very clever. You wouldn't like it." Then I listened again. It was dreadful. Somehow he was making the noise – like you can sometimes – of two people breathing.

"Stop it, Dan!"

His voice came from behind me. "What are you doing?"

My heart was nipped by a quick clawing hand. I slammed the receiver back into its little hook on the wall.

"Nothing."

It had not been Dan. And there had been two people breathing into the phone.

My reaction was to get angry. That kind of rage comes directly from fear sometimes. I allowed myself to admit it now: yes, I had heard footsteps in the night; and I was clear that the sounds I had heard coming from the speaking tube were not normal – and I wasn't having it.

"Come on, Dan," I said, and strode out of the kitchen.

"What? Where are you going?" He hurried after me, drawn on by my sense of purpose. Which vanished.

"I don't know." Or did I? Someone or something was teasing us. Through all my fear and anger I was sure of that much. I stood irresolute in the hall, Dan beside me.

I had no idea what made him say the thing he said next. It was as if he couldn't help saying it, I thought later – as if he had been prompted to say it.

"You were going to have another look in the attic, weren't you?" he said nervously. "I don't want to, Mandy."

Yes. Yes – I'd wanted to take action and that was something we could do, because there was a secret here somewhere and that trunk up there was the only clue we'd found and perhaps it was a clue we'd been *meant* to find, in some way.

"That's right, Dan. We're getting the lamps and we're going upstairs. We never saw what was in that trunk."

"What – now? It's dark, Mandy."

"I'll go by myself – I don't care." Then I spoke intentionally louder: "There's nothing to be afraid of!"

If I expected an answer from somewhere, none came. I spoke more softly again. "Nothing's going to happen. Nothing. You're not afraid, are you?"

"No – no. I'll come, but. . ."

But he didn't want to. And – I must be honest – my own courage ebbed away very fast. It was mostly vanity that carried me on. That, and the nagging suspicion that somehow we were supposed to find that trunk and go through it. . . And I began to understand how horror-film characters must feel when they're drawn to the places they should not visit.

We made an awful lot of noise going upstairs, stamping our feet down as if snakes had to be alerted to where we were and warned away.

In the top room I opened the attic door with a bang. Of course it only made the surrounding silence seem deeper and more ominous.

Tiptoeing unsteadily across the joists, the shafts of light from the lamps wavered wildly in our hands, casting darting shafts of light all around the loft space.

Our miniature searchlights found and held the dark bulk of the lead tank.

The top scraped back and there the wooden trunk sat. It wasn't very big but, being wood, it wasn't light either. I clambered in and wrestled with its awkwardness. The sounds were amplified by the tank and you felt that under cover of them someone could now easily creep up on you without being heard. . .

Between us we dragged and heaved at the trunk until it teetered on the edge of the tank. I got out while Dan held it balanced there and then we were able to carry it back the way we had come. Whatever else it held, it could not be a body, and for that I was grateful.

I went first down the narrow stairway to the top floor and Dan nearly let go and knocked me down with the trunk. We manhandled it down to our sitting room and turned on all the lights with a feeling of enormous relief at having got back to base.

It wasn't locked, but the two leather straps had hardened until they couldn't be budged. Keeping together for company, we went down to the kitchen and got the bread knife to use as a saw.

Twenty minutes later the lid came up, releasing a puff of dust and a musty smell of paper.

The trunk had been lined like a drawer, with patterned paper, and no damp had got in anywhere.

It was disappointing to see that it held so little; the weight of it had led me to expect more than just a few slim bundles of papers, tied with brittle, crumbling string.

Slowly, I untied the first packet of papers.

The cumululative effect of our reading was sombre in the extreme, though the papers didn't seem much at first, individually. What we had stumbled across were some remnants of the paperwork connected with running a home for the mentally unstable. There were laundry lists, old bills, and a collection of "receipts" (which I at last realized was an archaic way of saying "recipes") for wholesome and, by the sound of them, inexpensive meals made mostly from vegetables.

The bills were dated and so were some of the papers; those that were headed, Possessions on Arrival. The dates ranged between 1921 and 1929.

The possessions were few. For a Major Heatherington there was only: *pearl studs (full set, already discoloured); silver backed hair brush; one nightshirt & dressing gown.*

One definite "find" was a list of the rooms and their numbers, along with the names of the inhabitants of those rooms in January 1926.

The home had been called Lowlake Sanatorium and had housed around thirty mentally ill people, some sharing a room. What exactly they were suffering from we never found out, and possibly some of them were in any case diagnosed in a rough and ready fashion. Later I learned that women might be committed for life because they had had babies without being married – and that it was a mistake to become ill or cantankerous when you were old and rich and had unscrupulous relatives.

The names of the "residents" held a simple pathos: Mrs Drummond; Alfred Harcourt-Dawson; D. Cummings; Jack and Ethel Merriman. . .

We discovered that the sanatorium had a staff of only three and that their pay was so small as to make one wonder how well-qualified or caring they might have been. *Not very*, I thought to myself. *I'm glad I wasn't locked up here living off vegetables.*

But all this only filled in some details on what we knew already. Our most important discovery was a ground plan showing the layout of the house and garden. There had been more walls (and we had found the remains of some of these), and a herb garden as well as the formal back garden and the vegetable garden we had already guessed about. The lake was shown and the position of something called the Ice House. That was news to us, because these days there was no sign of a house or building where the Ice House was marked on the plan.

The paperwork from the sanatorium filled me with a kind of revulsion. This was meant to be our *home*.

Dan had an expression of disgust on his face too. "So," he said, "What do we do with these things?"

I didn't know. Once again I had not taken Dan into my confidence – about the alarming noises I had heard in the speaking tubes. If he didn't believe me there would be no point and it would be even worse if he did believe me. He would be a shivering mess.

Well, that's often the way when we think about those who are close to us; we don't give them credit for being as sensible or as brave as they really are.

"What are we going to do?" Dan repeated. "I don't want this in our house. None of it."

"Nor do I."

"And where's John?"

The mention of our father sparked off a sudden thought: *We were meant to find these things for him.* The idea that we were being used brought back the anger and the confusion in full spate. "I don't know and I don't care."

"Perhaps he didn't know about the lunatic asylum."

"Don't be stupid – of course he knew!" You couldn't have bought Lowlake and not have known about it. And now he was away when no decent parent would be. Leaving us to be scared by unseen presences in the house, leaving us to be directed to this horrible trunk. . .

Momentarily I had the sensation we were being watched. I shouted out, "Satisfied now? We found your precious trunk – now what?"

Dan was astonished. "It's not my precious trunk – it wasn't even my idea. I said – I don't even want it around!"

"It won't be. Not for much longer," I said grimly.

"Why – what do you mean?"

"We'll burn it. That'll show them." Again I raised my voice, "How do you like *that*?"

Not a clever idea. But I just had to express the fury I was feeling. There was, too, a primeval need to destroy the unknown, the object that causes fear. Like a wild savage might break up a camera, precisely because it's a mystery to him. So, all worked up like I was, I went with the hope that if we destroyed the trunk we'd be getting rid of some of the spookiness of the house. I even tried to tell myself that maybe it was what we were meant to do too, but really I knew I was frightened and wanted to lash out. I hoped it would make John angry too, when he found out. He wasn't playing fair with us and I was going to be as irresponsible as I liked. And it would be his fault. Not mine – *his*.

Even so, I took every precaution I could think of. I decided the safest place for the fire was near the old lake, where it was wet. I would use some white spirit to make sure the fire got going – but only a very little. What with all the painting and decorating there was gallons of the stuff available – but I wouldn't go overboard with it. And – proving very satisfactorily

to myself that I was being reasonable about all this –
I wasn't going to burn the map of the grounds either
. . . only all the horrible stuff about the asylum.

In the darkness we set the trunk down near the
boggy land and I sprinkled white spirit on it. I had
a rolled-up newspaper to use as a torch. It had been
very windy but as I prepared the fire the wind
dropped right down to nothing and let in the
quietness of the big open spaces.

It was a distinctive hush. Different. . .

Disapproving.

I ploughed right on, though my fingers were
shaking when I lit the newspaper taper.

The trunk, primed with white spirit, caught
alight with a blue flame so pale and insubstantial
that it looked like the kind of flame you see on a
Christmas pudding when "the big moment" comes
and is such a let-down.

The blue flames flickered over the old wood with
no real interest in it and then, in the sudden way
fire has, they took hold and turned yellow and
vicious. Within a very short space of time the trunk
was ablaze. The wind got up again and fed the
conflagration with oxygen and it got very dramatic,
dancing brightly under the night sky.

That was when John turned up. We saw the
lights of the Landrover jouncing over the little rise,
pointing upwards for a moment, and there it was,
coming down towards us.

We weren't looking at the fire at that moment and in an instant there was the most tremendous gust of wind which fanned the blaze right at us – like a fire-eater blowing flame at us, but with intent to hurt. Dan pulled me back sharply and I fell over and got angry all over again.

Not as angry as John. The brakes on the Landrover protested as he slammed the jeep to a halt. He was running to us, his face livid with fury in the firelight.

"What do you think you're doing?"

6

"I can't leave you for a minute!" he said.

"It was a lot more than that – where've you been?" Dan retorted aggressively.

"What is that?"

He meant what were we burning.

"It's an old trunk we found," I said, trying to be calm.

"Where? Where did you find it?"

"In the attic. It had a whole lot of old papers in it."

"What? Why didn't you tell me!"

"Because you weren't here!" Dan shouted.

John looked at the fire and took a step towards it, then he ran over to the Landrover.

"Now what?" Dan asked.

John came running back with a tyre wrench. He went as close to the fire as he could and poked the wrench into the side of the trunk. It crumbled in an outrush of sparks. But John was now able to get a purchase on the trunk and could pull at it. The whole side of the trunk came away and the rest collapsed into a burning mass.

Using his foot, John dragged smouldering fragments of wood out of the flames. He took off his jacket and used it as a fire blanket to save what he could of the trunk. It wasn't much. We watched in dumb amazement. He would need a new jacket now.

When he had done all he could he became conscious of how we were looking at him.

"There might have been something important in it," he said defensively.

"There wasn't. We looked," I said.

"I don't understand you. Playing with matches! It's dangerous! Why would you want to burn it in the first place?"

Right. Time to attack.

"We didn't like finding records of how this place used to be a loony bin," I said in a hard voice.

"I'm very disappointed in you," was all he said and that made Dan lose his temper completely.

"You didn't tell us! We had a right to know! It's horrible, living in a lunatic asylum! You didn't dare tell us – and you left us alone here for hours! At night! Is that what parents are meant to do? Don't you dare go on about us being dangerous!"

John shut his face up tight, in the same way Dan did when things weren't going his way.

He said with terrible slowness, "I had things I had to do. Things I had to get. And I went to see your grandmother. It all took more time than I had expected. Then I had a puncture in the middle of nowhere. Satisfied?"

"You didn't phone," I said.

That had him. He stuttered, "I was in a hurry to get here – that was why. I wanted to, but – there wasn't a phone . . . I. . ."

"There's a phone at Gran's nursing home."

"All right," he said icily, "I've had enough of your impertinence. Now go to your rooms. Right now."

At that moment he was the army officer; not a man to argue with. I took hold of Dan's sleeve, willing him to keep his mouth shut, because whatever the rights and wrongs of it this scene had gone quite far enough.

I said, "OK," and I led Dan away. We turned back after a few steps and already John seemed to have forgotten about us. At some cost to his hands he was examining the smouldering fragments of the trunk. It appeared that between the charred lining and the wood he had spotted something; he gently pulled out a fragment of paper.

"Barking mad," Dan said. "This is the right place for him."

"What kept him away so long? What was he getting that was so important?" I wondered aloud. He wasn't looking at us so we took a detour to pass by the Landrover. You couldn't see much inside. It must have been at least eleven o'clock at night now. There were a few boxes, that much I could make out. And on top of them was a dirty old glass case with two stuffed ducks inside, with blind bead eyes.

"That was what he wanted?" Dan said incredulously.

An hour later John came up the stairs. Softly and, I sensed, perhaps apologetically.

"Amanda?" he said gently. "Are you awake?"

"Yes."

"Dan?"

"Yes thanks." There was no forgiveness in Dan's voice.

"Well, come into Amanda's room, will you. I want to talk."

I turned my bedside light on and first John, and then Dan came in and we all sat on my bed before John started talking.

"You were quite right. You haven't done anything wrong. Of course not. I was the one who wasn't behaving properly and I'm sorry." He waited for our generous acceptance of his generous apology and it didn't happen.

"I haven't been a father for very long – not a proper one. So I hope you'll make some allowances for that. Perhaps I should have told you about Lowlake being a – well, being the kind of institution it was – but I knew it'd put you off and by the time I found out about it I was completely sold on the house. Everything about it seems right. I'm not psychic or anything, but I get such a happy feeling here. A feeling that this is the right place to bring up a family. Don't you feel that?"

"No," I said bluntly.

"I think it feels horrible," Dan added.

"You're wrong. I just know it. And, for heaven's sake, this is an old house. It was only a place for ill people for a short while in its life – for just a few years in the 1920s. The rest of the time it's been a happy place. I'd swear to it. You couldn't feel like I do about Lowlake and be wrong about it."

I saw that his hands were red and burnt and that he had put moisturizer on them as an ointment. "Was it worth getting yourself burnt, for the things in the trunk?"

"That was silly of me, wasn't it. But I did find something interesting."

"What?" Dan asked.

"A bit of a letter. A nice letter. I'll read it to you

in the morning. And we'll have some more fun soon, too. I promise. All right?"

The next morning we had breakfast together. It was all very homey – making coffee and toast, and hot chocolate (for Dan), and sitting at a kitchen table with the smell of the cooking still in the room.

Afterwards, John read us the letter he'd found stuffed down the side of the trunk and I kind of wished we hadn't burnt it after all. He was enthusiastic, saying, "It's a loving letter. No doubt written to a couple of people who were in the sanatorium just because they were a little simple-minded."

I thought callously, *Or because they were a couple of complete raving loonies who were a danger to themselves and everyone else.*

John said without rancour, "I can't see the date, because of you two. Anyway. . ." He read: " '*My dear ones, it has been such a long time, but at last I shall soon be with you again and –*' the next bit's scorched – '*The –*' it looks like '*Wanatan*' . . . no, it's '*the Waratan*' I think – '*will be calling at Africa, but merely to take on –*' I think it's fuel – '*and passengers, so. . .*' No – can't read the next bit. Anyway, '*I trust you no longer feel as though you were in prison, as you suggested in your dear letter. Surely it is a fantasy for you to believe that any letter from you must be "smuggled out", as you put it? Regarding these nightmares you describe, I truly believe such dreams are only to be . . . when one considers. . .'* Fascinating, isn't it? The bottom of it's gone, unfortunately."

"It doesn't sound like the people who were locked up in Lowlake thought it was a happy house," Dan said, sticking to his guns.

"They would have been confused. Probably feeling the effects of their illness and medication and things. But the letter clearly comes from a caring person."

John put it on the table. I reached out for it and a breeze took it away from me.

It scampered back towards John.

We had the window open because of the cooking and there was a breeze, but even so the paper seemed to have a life of its own. John didn't comment, but put his hand on the letter to stop it moving, and it – well – I can only say it settled down again.

Then Mrs Martindale arrived with her husband and our little family get-together was interrupted. While John greeted her at the door Dan said, "I wonder what he's done with those dead ducks. . ."

We went to what we now thought of as "John's Room", the library at the end of the house.

The door was locked. Dan bent down to look through the keyhole and almost immediately John's voice said, "It's a secret, but not very!"

He stood at the bottom of the stairs, smiling

warmly. "I'll let you see inside when I've finished and not before. It's going to be really special. A wonderful place to work in – when I get started!"

He went upstairs to shave and Dan said, "He's got the other side blocked. I mean, you can't see through the keyhole."

"Well, we'll see it when he's ready," I said with a cheerfulness we both knew was false.

We didn't know it, but somewhere during the course of that day is when we should have acted – should have *done* something or at least talked to someone of our worries about Lowlake.

But the moment passed without us realizing that the opportunity to talk to anyone was going to disappear when Mrs Martindale's husband came to pick her up at lunchtime.

I wandered into my room when she was in there with the Hoover. The brand-new vacuum cleaner made an awful row which sounded incredibly efficient, and though I wanted to ask Mrs Martindale what she thought about Lowlake, I didn't. She was efficient herself, with an I-don't-want-to-be-distracted-from-my-work attitude implicit in her every movement. And she wouldn't look at me. As I had noticed before, she did not encourage conversation of any kind.

So I wandered out again.

Dan was sitting on the front step trying to make

a catapult with a stick and a rubber band. He said, "You can't see in from the outside. He keeps the shutters closed."

"Oh leave it alone," I said sharply. "We're getting ourselves worked up for no reason."

"You think so?"

I didn't answer.

Dan tried out his catapult. "Hopeless", he said. "Hey – John's taking us out after lunch. That'll be good, anyway."

"Where to?"

"He didn't say."

"Oh. Wouldn't you just know it."

"He said it was another magical mystery trip."

"It's all mystery with him," I said sourly.

Lunch came and went and shortly afterwards Mrs Martindale went, too. Her little husband waited for her by his car. Very close to his car, you couldn't help but notice.

Mrs Martindale came out of the house briskly (no-time-for-goodbyes-if-I-want-to get-my-shopping–done) and stumped rapidly to Mr Martindale.

I ran over to them.

"Well – goodbye Mrs Martindale. See you on Friday."

"No you won't. Be good, and look after your brother."

She said that with prim satisfaction and got herself all neat beside her husband in the front of the car. He only smiled at me tepidly, not really looking.

And then they were off, pulling away from Lowlake at quite a lick.

I asked John what she had meant about not coming on Friday. He said, "Why – don't you think other people deserve holidays too?"

"She's taking a holiday, is she?"

"Only a couple of weeks. We'll manage somehow, won't we? If we all muck in!"

Shortly afterwards we three got into our car too and accelerated away.

John wouldn't be drawn on where we were going. He said casually, "I had thought of looking in on your grandmother, but then I decided to pop in yesterday, so I don't think we need to. She was happy to hear about you and how well we're getting on."

"It would be nice to see her," I remarked brightly, disguising a stab of worry. Suddenly it seemed it would be a good idea to talk to Gran and I wanted to promote the idea.

Dan wasn't having it. "Not today. She's all right. John's only just been there."

He was excited about the mystery trip. My stab of worry had been that, with Mrs Martindale gone and Gran not expecting a visit, we were rather marooned now. There was only us and John and he was – well – so preoccupied. I would have quite liked a word with Gran and it had somehow been denied me. Would it be fair on her to tell her of my doubts about Lowlake over the phone? No, and in any case all I'd get back was her usual common sense. . .

Thinking of the phone brought the speaking-tube to mind. I tried to remember what the voice in it had sounded like, but I could only bring back the sensation of fear I had experienced. All the time the knowledge was growing that Lowlake harboured something unpleasant. Or, at least, something beyond normal rules or reason. Clearly John wouldn't take me seriously about any of that. . .

And Dan? In trying to protect him from the worst of my fears, was I doing both of us no favours? Actually, part of it was a stubborn refusal to give in to panic. Along with that went my foolish pride about not looking stupid.

In my mind I could hear Gran saying, as she had once when I had lost my temper with her, "Young girls of your age are prone to sudden and distressing emotions and feelings, and they have no understanding of them and no control over them. It's just a part of growing up. I'm glad I'm not young any more!"

No, talking to Gran most likely wouldn't have helped much. I kept quiet and looked out of the window.

It was probably my imagination but the further we got from Lowlake the warmer it seemed to get.

After quite some time Dan said, outraged, "This is the way to Derby – we're going to Derby!"

"I'm afraid that is where the mystery trip leads us, yes," John said with a private grin.

"That's not very exciting!"

"Oh, I think we'll enjoy ourselves. I was all over the country yesterday, finding more things for the house – and I found some places which just might interest you two as well. You see, I'm going to be busy, writing my book and things, and I want to make sure you have some jolly good entertainment too."

All my instincts said, in one rush, *He's buying us off*.

It was one of those realizations that one forgets in a moment or two.

But he was.

And it worked quite brilliantly.

For openers, Dan was taken to a hunting-and-shooting shop which was seventh heaven to him. He wasn't allowed a gun but he did get a thoroughly dangerous crossbow and a factory-made metal catapult whose packaging proclaimed, "This is not a toy!" Best of all was a clasp-knife so beautiful that I at once wanted one myself.

And was bought one.

For a girl there were other delights. Hair dryer, curling tongs, magazines, make-up of every kind I could think of to buy. These were the things we chose for ourselves. John had his own ideas for us. I didn't mind the painting sets he got us – both water-colours and oils, in big boxes – but his other choices seemed quaintly old-fashioned. Talk about making your own entertainment. He bought jigsaws and board-games and card-games. Even a papier-maché modelling set and a set of wooden skittles! We indulged him and then dragged him off to find more modern goodies. Trainers so light and bouncy they seemed to do your walking for you. Designer label clothes which combined fashion and comfort at premium prices. Some CDs for me, more games cartridges for Dan, *and* the new Playstation games he wanted – as well as a portable television for upstairs just for use with the Playstation. . .

If in the midst of our shopping frenzy we had stopped to think we would have seen so clearly that each and every one of these lovely new possessions was telling us that we were going to be left to our own devices for hours or whole days at a time.

But John was loving and gentle and considerate and seemed to take such pleasure in our pleasure; it was impossible not to be charmed by him as well as the things he was giving us.

Dan was peacocking around in his first leather

jacket, in front of the mirror in the shop. It wasn't even as though he'd have much use for it, till Autumn.

"You're a man now," John joked flatteringly.

And I was a girl in a tank top Gran would have quietly hated. I looked terrific, no doubt about it.

However, in the Landrover, on the long drive back to Lowlake, I felt depressed suddenly. Dan was still on a big high, but I was feeling a sick reaction to surfeit, like when you pig out on sweets. We had been given too much. While our first great shopping expedition had seemed spontaneous, this one had been, in a weird way, counterfeit.

Now, all around us in the jeep were all these wonderful things in their boxes, and inside me was this empty feeling.

A kind of desolation.

As we got nearer Lowlake it seemed, inexplicably, that the temperature dropped again.

7

Exhausted by our riches, we went to bed thoroughly bemused. On getting them home, even I had been unable to resist the thrill of all the desirable objects and we had acted out some kind of imitation Christmas Day in our sitting room; setting up the TV so Dan could give the new games the once-over; gloating over the brilliance of our new belongings and being restrained in our jokes about the old-fashioned stuff John had got us – until eventually he had called us down to supper.

After we had eaten we left John in the kitchen, where he was tranquilly listening to a comedy show on the radio, and dashed back up to continue the fondling of all the lovely things.

Then the tiredness and the empty feeling hit us both.

We were ashamed of glorying in our possessions and yet the luxury of them made it impossible to talk of anything else, so we both staggered off to bed in silence.

Even so, just as if we had talked about Lowlake, we both slept with the light on in our rooms.

I was lying there and I knew we'd been fooled somehow – that having all the goodies was a diversion. You got so confused, though, having wonderful things of your very own for almost the first time in your life. . . The kind of things you would envy some other kid for having. . .

I'll think about it all properly in the morning, I thought vaguely.

Sleep came up from a long way below and dragged me down.

I was in Gran's front room, only it was bigger and full of bookshelves. Gran was in her chair watching television, only the set wasn't on.

John stood in front of me where I sat on a hard chair by the door. He had a long overcoat on with a tiny collar and his hands were grasped in the lapels as if he was a barrister in court, presenting a case.

"My dear," he said in an un-John-like way, "I wish it could be otherwise."

I didn't answer. I was a witness in this dream more than a character in her own right.

He lowered his head to ponder something. "We don't, in this life, always have the choices we would like to have. I must go away, you must stay."

Something funny was happening with the floor. It was tilting. John seemed to be having trouble keeping his balance. Gran just went on looking at the blank TV screen.

"I will think of you every day," John said, raising his voice against the wind which had begun to buffet the house furiously. "Think of me too. We shall be together, though apart. We will always be together. I love you very much."

The television slid across the floor and banged into the wall. Gran stayed where she was.

"Behave yourselves and be grateful for what you have," John shouted and the windows burst and a wall of sea water engulfed us.

I woke up.

Dan had set up an old door against the garden wall and was shooting crossbow bolts at it. They stuck in very satisfactorily.

"Look at that grouping," he said, fixated (I imagined) by the fantasy of being a top performer in a crossbow shooting event – if there was such a sport.

"Let's have a go," I said.

"No."

John was hoovering. Everything was normal. Dan and me went for a walk later and Dan took his catapult.

"Kill a rabbit easily with this," he said.

I wondered if John had thought at all about the suitability of the things he had given us. In his rush to keep us happy he had bought whatever we had lusted for. After an early lunch he pottered around the house and we got stuck into Monopoly. Dan was getting this thing that we had to do things together all the time and Playstation games never appealed to me. It came as a mild surprise that Monopoly was fun to play. It's one of those games that can get to you, which is why it's lasted so long, I suppose.

Some hours later we were on our second game. Dan had insisted, because he'd lost the first.

I was stuck – trying to work out whether I could afford to put another house on Park Lane and still get round the board safely – when I became aware of that expectant silence creeping into the house again.

"What's the time?" I asked absently.

Dan looked at his new wristwatch. "Three o'clock."

"Where's John?" I was only making conversation.

"In his room. I think."

He was. You just knew it from that silence.

He had pacified us with the presents and by being available for us and now he was allowing himself to get on with his own thing. Writing his book.

In a locked room.

"I had a dream after we got back from Derby — you know, the other night," I said.

Most dreams somehow reflect your own experiences and fears in some ghastly distorted way, but that one had seemed to contain more. I had the oddest notion that Dan might have had the same dream.

"It was really strange," I said.

"I had a peculiar dream too, that night," Dan said, remembering. "It was ever so vivid."

"Really?"

"Yeah. I thought I was in Africa or somewhere and then there was this lion and it was going to eat me."

"Oh."

I told him about my dream. I finished with, "But they don't mean anything, do they, dreams?"

"No. Shall we get on with the game?"

"No, I don't think so. Later, maybe."

"All right."

"Don't want to get sick of it, do we?"

"No."

A little pause . . . and then we started speaking at the same time. I said, "You remember that map?"

and Dan said, "We could have a look for that Ice House place."

I had kept the map at the bottom of a drawer in my room. The Ice House was marked as being at the end of the garden, in a corner.

Dan and I struggled through the long grass and weeds.

He said, "I lost one of my bolts – we might find that too."

"It's the Ice House we're going to find," I said firmly.

"Yes. Yes – of course."

He was uneasy now. We went to the corner where the Ice House should have been. Or would have been, once.

"Well," Dan said with some relief, "There's nothing here now."

"We haven't looked yet," I snapped in irritation.

Arriving at where the garden walls met in a neat corner, we looked. The bricks, though old, did not appear to have been disturbed. If there had once been a building set here you would have expected the bricks there to look different in some way.

"Let's get a spade," I said. "Wouldn't it have had foundations?"

"Dunno."

We went back to the house for a spade and returned along the path we had trampled.

We took turns in digging and I'm sure we did the garden a lot of good. . .

All we turned up was soil and plant roots. The Ice House, judging by the map, had only been about the size of a summer house, so there wasn't any point in digging in a bigger arc.

We were sweating: it was a low, close day, threatening rain. The more sure I became that we would find nothing the more sure I was that the Ice House had some extraordinary importance.

Dan saw I wouldn't give up without prompting, so he grumbled, "Oh come on. This is hopeless. Maybe the map was wrong – or it was just a shed or something. If you want to do something useful you can help me look for my bolt."

That seemed even more of a fruitless exercise than looking for the remnants of an old building, so I left Dan to it and went back to the house. I listened to a CD track with the volume set low and the music was so modern and right now and normal that thoughts of the house being strange began to seem foolish and hysterical. Only when the track finished did I think of my brother all by himself out there, and the idea of it got to me a little. Turning off the sound system, I went into an empty room which overlooked the back garden – I was going to call to Dan, so we could get on with the Monopoly.

There he was, plodding through the weeds with his head down, looking oddly small because I was so much higher up. The perspective was different from here and something began to nag at me. I took the crumpled map out of my pocket.

Yes. The garden appeared longer on the map than the actual one was outside. And at this angle one noticed very clearly that, down there, the end wall was slightly lighter in colour and the bricks just a fraction smaller. . .

I ran back downstairs and rejoined Dan.

"They rebuilt the whole wall," I said breathlessly. "They made the garden shorter!"

By walking the length of the end wall one got an idea of the scale of the map and we could guess with some certainty that the original wall would have been about ten metres further back. The element of detective work had fuelled us with excitement and so we threw the spade over the wall and climbed after it with enthusiasm.

Within ten minutes we had found the Ice House.

First we found the line of the original side-walls: some of the bricks were still there at foundation level. The problem was in finding just how long the garden had been originally and it was longer than we had estimated it to be. With that established, we went to the corner where the Ice House should have been, and dug.

And struck stone slabs about thirty centimetres beneath the surface.

It was gone tea-time – always an important time of day for Dan – but we dug on furiously, taking turns with the spade and using our hands as well. They got raw and blistered.

We uncovered an area of stone paving the size and shape of a small square room. It told us nothing. That was what we should have expected – but we were desperately disappointed.

"What a waste of time!" Dan complained. "A floor. Very exciting."

"Don't blame me – you wanted to find it too."

It began to rain, big warm drops.

"That's it." Dan got up from where he was kneeling and turned away without a backward glance, calling over his shoulder, "Time to press the buttons!" He meant he was going on the Playstation, and he went off chanting like at a football match, "Stay-shu-un. . . Stay-shu-un. . ."

I got up slowly. The rain came down more strongly, as if a tap had been opened wider. It washed down on the slabs beneath my trainers, clearing earth from between them.

As I went to follow Dan, one of the slabs moved. Only a fraction, but it definitely shifted under my weight.

I didn't bother calling Dan back for what would probably be another disappointment. Using the spade I levered up the slab, almost as a matter of duty, having got this far.

The rain beat down on dirt and dull metal. Someone had hidden a box under the old Ice House. A dark thing made of rusting metal. The corners were incredibly sharp, but I was careful.

It wasn't locked. I couldn't wait, and lifted the lid. It rasped in warning as it came off.

"Mandy! Mandy! What – what?"

Dan was running back. He had been watching me from the shelter of the house.

I was already examining the contents . . . a much smaller box made of stainless steel. Some things wrapped in a greasy covering I later found out was called oilcloth.

Dan was at my side.

"Here." I handed him the smaller metal box to open and unwrapped the oilcloth package. Inside was a curly-stemmed wooden pipe, a paper folder with printed songs inside, and a picture in a brass frame. The brass was green with verdigris.

Dan was having trouble with the little box, which wouldn't open. I turned the picture round to look at it.

It was a sepia representation of a man. You couldn't tell if it was a photograph or not, but it was very realistic. He stood with his hand resting on a writing table; a tall man in a long black jacket. He had a moustache and beard. He carried his head high and under the beard you could see that the white collar he wore was stiff and uncomfortable.

He looks like John, I thought, and said aloud, faintly: "This. . . He looks quite like John, don't you think?"

Dan dropped the stainless steel box. "Let me see. Oh . . . yes. A bit."

"More than a bit."

"What's in the folder?"

I looked. "Old songs . . . 'Only a Bird in a Gilded Cage' . . . 'Just a Song at Twilight' ."

That didn't interest Dan, who went back to wrestling with the box.

We should have got the things into the dry. It was too exciting, though. I turned the folder over.

Someone had scrawled in pen all over the back, in large letters, *"Cursed be thee that uncovers me."*

As rain softened the old paper and its smudged curse I heard Dan let out a high noise of shock and intense pain.

Blood was spurting from his hand, dark red at its source, washing down his arm in pinker streams as it mingled with the rainwater.

8

"What's an Ice House anyway?"

Dan was paler than the cloth he had wrapped tight around his hand and had the nervous energy of someone who has just had a pretty big shock.

John drove the Landrover fast, going to the doctor's surgery in Essop. I sat in the back. John had said I didn't have to come but there was no way I wanted to be left alone at Lowlake.

Besides, I had the thought that it wouldn't be such a bad idea to make contact with the doctor. My instinct said we might need some adult help if things got even weirder around our new house and – I felt guilty for even thinking it – I had a horrible suspicion that John was not going to be of much use to us. He had not answered Dan's question just now; was staring fixedly at the road ahead. Still, I knew he had been badly worried about Dan's injury because he'd been so frantically cross about it.

In the steel box had been an old-fashioned, 'cut-throat' razor and, not knowing what it was, Dan had opened the blade out and cut himself in one easy movement. John came running when I called and dealt with the wound as best he could. Despite all the hurry and worry he had also asked me to bring with us the things we had found, so he could have a look at them when he got a moment.

His silence had come down on us all when he saw the picture of the man with a beard.

Now Dan repeated himself querulously: "I said, what's an Ice House?"

"Sorry?" John roused himself from the deep.

"We thought that place was called the Ice House."

"Oh. Yes – there would have been one, probably."

"But what is it?"

"Before fridges they had these small buildings which were cold enough to store ice in. If you were quite well-off."

"Oh. Seems a funny place to keep things."

I came in with, "Not if you were hiding them. Then it might be a very good place. Someone was hiding something very special. It was like a little shrine."

"Don't talk nonsense," John said curtly. "That's your imagination at work."

"There is something so odd about Lowlake," Dan blurted out.

"No there isn't. You're a couple of hysterics."

Our local GP was a little younger than John and thought rather a lot of himself (it seemed to me). I don't suppose it was his fault. In a small community the only doctor has great standing.

Dr Hawthorne wasn't much good with young people, either. You could tell that when he said Dan was a "brave old chap". Later he said I was a brave old girl too: we were both given tetanus injections after he had put three stitches in Dan's hand and had examined the blisters and broken skin on mine.

But even though he wasn't easy to talk to I hoped to get a word with the doctor alone, to talk about Lowlake. John stayed with us both all the time though, so eventually I thought I'd better just get on with it. I'd just started off with a casual, "About Lowlake. . ." when John grabbed me by the arm – the arm that had been injected – and started talking rapidly to shut me up. That was certainly how it appeared to me. He spoke of how busy a GP must be in a place like Essop and kept talking and talking and got us out of the little surgery as fast as he could.

He got us out of Essop fast too. It really was like he didn't want us to speak to anyone at all. I pleaded for another browse in Mr Burton's bookshop, but John only snapped, "Haven't I bought you enough already?"

Which was so unfair.

Except that, in a way, he was right to mistrust me if he didn't want us talking to anyone about Lowlake. Passing the bookshop, I realized that, with all the books in there about the Peak District, old and new, the shop and its owner, old Mr Burton, would be far and away the best source of information about our house. The unworthy suspicion popped into my head that John had deliberately made sure we never got to talk to Gran ... just as he hadn't told us that Mrs Martindale was going to be away. But after all, there was no special reason why he should tell us when Mrs Martindale was taking a holiday. Only now we were, well, totally marooned up there at Lowlake.

I badly wanted a chance to study in more detail the things we had dug up, but as we got out of the car back at Lowlake (so very quickly returned there), John said brusquely, "I'll look after these," and virtually confiscated what we had found.

So here we were, back in our prison.

It was, so far, an open prison, and crammed with well-chosen diversions, but a prison nonetheless.

John went back into his room and locked the door.

If we were prisoners, then so was he, in some other kind of way.

There we were, back in our sitting room, with the movie posters and the best micro sound system money could buy, and our unfinished game of Monopoly littering the floor.

There we were, back with the silence.

"What are we going to do?" Dan pleaded and I knew he didn't mean what to do to pass the time.

I couldn't think of a single thing to say.

After a moment Dan gave me a contemptuous look and settled himself in the one armchair, to look at his book of *One Hundred and One Wonders for Boys*, turning the pages fast like you do with a magazine, but clumsily because of his stitched-up hand. He'd got fond of the book in the time he'd had it. Something to laugh at. There wasn't much else round here to lighten your spirits.

I got down on my hands and knees and swept up the Monopoly pieces and put them back in the box with the gameboard. Then I sorted through my CD and mini-disc collections, arranging them each in alphabetical order, which didn't take long.

When I looked up there were two people standing behind Dan, just to one side of him. Smiling.

They were old and plump and soft, and see-through, like they were made of fine grains of sand which didn't quite join.

The man wore corduroy trousers and a shirt without a collar and, improbably, a businessman's blue pin-striped waistcoat. He was smiling with his mouth open, a pendulous bottom lip drooping wetly. His arm was round the woman's waist.

She was wearing a shapeless pale dress, tied at the waist with string. She had sharper features protruding from her wrinkled face, but the eyes were faded and dull and she had the same meaningless smile.

They looked at me and smiled.

How long we stared at each other I don't know. Their immobility was not reassuring. Rather, it suggested that at any moment they might make a sudden movement.

"Dan," I said, conversationally, with my heart pounding so hard that it felt like my chest would burst, "Dan. . ."

"What." He examined my face. "What?"

"I, um. . ."

The old people stood beside and just behind him and their smiles seemed to take on a sinister life, with a worrying kind of inner delight glowing through.

"Listen, Dan," I said firmly, with no idea of what to say next.

"I am. What is it?"

"There's . . . I've got something to show you."

I didn't mean the two apparitions. All I wanted to do was to get Dan – and me – away from them. Without terrifying my younger brother.

"What is it?"

He was getting to his feet, glad of the distraction. I turned my back on him and left the room at what I hoped was a normal pace. I no longer had any idea of how one moved or spoke normally. I did know that, having roused his curiosity, my disappearing back would draw him on to follow.

And he did. He came after me into the corridor and I shut the door behind us rather fast, with only a split second in which to see that the two soft old people were still there with their smiles and their togetherness.

"So – what is it?"

"What?"

"What you're going to show me."

"Oh. Yes, I. . ." My mind went into neutral, spinning wildly, empty of ideas. "I thought. . ."

"There isn't anything. What are you up to?"

Something came to me at last. "I thought we'd have a look at what John's doing!"

"What d'you mean – knock on the door?"

"No – just have a look."

"We can't – you can't see. It's blocked off."

"I bet we could see if we tried."

Dan trotted after me into my bedroom, enthused by the energy in my voice. Fear and worry was coming off me like static, but he thought it was excitement because I'd thought of something to do.

I took an unlikely lock-picking tool from my bedside table and we went downstairs. I didn't even look towards our sitting room.

The shutters were shut and the door was locked, as usual.

Insert a nail file ever so gently in the keyhole. Work it around. Something metal was the obstruction. Try pushing. . .

Of course – it's the key itself, I thought, *Gosh I'm stupid! And what that means is . . . if it were to drop out of the keyhole there would be quite some noise when it hit the floor.*

It was just as I'd had the thought that the key fell – and I flinched back nervously.

We heard a dull clatter and then the only sound was that of our breathing as we knelt outside the door, our heads poised by the keyhole. I tensed, ready to run when John came to the door. The idea that I wanted to run from my own father was frightening in itself.

Nothing happened.

"He's not there," Dan whispered hoarsely.

"He must be."

I wondered if I would see much when I looked in. Even though it was a large keyhole my field of vision would be severely restricted.

I put my eye to the keyhole. John was looking right at me.

He was sitting rigidly in a tall armchair beside his leather-topped writing table, facing the door. A little way behind him was a low table with an old-fashioned gramophone on it. In his lap he held the yellowing sheet music of "Only a Bird in a Gilded Cage".

He was looking straight towards me and he couldn't see anything. His face was dead and vacant.

He was just sitting there. Not writing a book; not doing anything.

It was horrible.

"My turn!" Dan whispered excitedly. He pushed me aside and took his place at the spy-hole. He stayed there, looking, for several seconds.

He turned to me with panic on his face. "What's he doing?"

"Nothing."

"I don't like it, Mandy." His voice was loud and whiny with fear and distress.

"I don't like it either," I said.

"He's ill, isn't he?"

"Something like that. Sort of, maybe."

"What are we going to do?"

"I'm not sure," I said slowly.

"What about the doctor?"

"I don't know if it's that kind of illness."

Dan began knocking on the door. "John. John. John!"

I pushed him aside and knelt to look through the keyhole again. John had not moved a muscle.

"Well." I said. "He's been in there a lot. But he always comes out eventually, doesn't he?"

"You mean we should just wait?" You could tell Dan was too upset to exercise any patience.

"I don't think we have to disturb him."

"But what do we do? You don't mean we should just go upstairs and play games, or listen to CDs?"

"No," I said quickly. I didn't want to go back into our sitting room – not yet – not ever again, maybe.

I tried to think. Suddenly it seemed terribly unfair that all this should be put on me – that I was the one who was supposed to take all the decisions. I wanted some adult assistance, if there was any to be had. Not Gran. She was *too* old . . . but . . . And I thought of Mr Burton.

"Let's go somewhere. On the bikes," I said. "We'll go and see Mr Burton in his shop. I wanted to when we went to the doctor, but we didn't get the chance."

"Yes. All right. We'll tell him about John, will we?"

"I don't know about that. Perhaps. It's the house, Dan. You know it is."

He was silent.

"You know it is, Dan."

"Yes," he said reluctantly.

"We'll see what we can find out about it."

"And we'll get Mr Burton to help us." He just wouldn't let go of the thought that a grown-up could be brought in to fix things.

"Yes, I suppose we will." I sounded fairly certain about that, but I wasn't.

Two minutes later we were pedalling away from Lowlake. Rain clouds populated the sky above us and it felt later than it was.

I'm sure it was the rapid motion that made me think that something was watching us from behind. Like when you start to walk fast at night – as soon as you do you're more sure than ever there's something or someone behind you.

"Don't go so fast," Dan panted. "I can't keep up."

I slowed the bike down. It took a conscious act of courage to do it.

In Essop the shops were shutting for the day. Dan and I swept up to Mr Burton's shop and propped up the bikes against the window. The sign said OPEN and we went in.

There were shelves floor-to-ceiling all around the

walls, all crammed with books, and there were big free-standing bookcases down the middle of the shop too. Stacks of books and old magazines lay on the floor here and there.

Mr Burton was not behind the tiny table by the door. The door rang a bell, though, so I supposed he must have heard us come in.

Labels showing the categories of book were sellotaped to the shelves. "Travel", "Philosophy", "History". I was more agitated than I thought I was, because I couldn't remember where I'd seen the books on the local area.

"Was there anything special?"

I smelled stale tobacco smoke before Mr Burton materialized as if by magic from behind one of the central bookcases.

"Oh. Hello."

"Hello." The wet, growly voice was intimidating.

"We, er, we were looking for some books," I volunteered foolishly.

"You're in the right place then." He smiled encouragingly.

"It's our house," Dan said.

"Yes," I went on quickly. "We wanted to know a bit more about it. And the whole area too, of course. But mostly the house."

"You're up at Lowlake, aren't you?"

"Yes. And, well – it's been there a long time, hasn't it? We thought it must have a history."

His eyes narrowed with a quick interest. "What sort of history do you mean?"

"Just because it's old . . . that's all," I stammered.

"Anyway, you want to know about Lowlake."

"Yes."

"You're still in the right place, then," Mr Burton rumbled. "Come on through."

We followed him towards the back of the shop.

He said, "I know quite a lot about Lowlake."

9

Mr Burton's back room was as cluttered as his shop. It had one long window where daylight struggled through an amber-coloured blind that had once been yellow. Tobacco smoke curled up from a crowded ashtray on the low wooden table in front of his beaten-down sofa.

"So. Lowlake. . ."

Mr Burton pulled up a chair, took out a packet of cigarettes and lit up, oblivious to the butt smouldering in the ashtray. We realized that we had been granted the sofa and sat down. It was a bit like an informal meeting with one's headmaster.

I said carelessly, "Of course we know it was a mental institution."

"Oh it's been a lot of things, Lowlake, for a lot of people. None of them had much luck."

"What do you mean?"

"Failed enterprises. Hardly surprising. You're very remote up there. It's been a farm, mostly, but not much of one. It was built by a Bluejohn miner. He went bust at the end. But the house was there to stay."

"Yes?" I encouraged politely.

"You know about Bluejohn, do you?"

"No."

"It's a local stone. Had quite a vogue. I've got some books about it, if you're interested." He looked hopeful.

"It was the sanatorium we were most interested in."

An expression of contempt passed across Mr Burton's face and he drew on his cigarette dismissively. "Oh. Well, I suppose you would be. The sensational period of the house's history. That would appeal to the adolescent mind."

Dan broke in with his usual vehemence, "I don't think the idea of living in a mental institution would appeal to anyone."

"It isn't one now, young man. That was years ago."

"Even so," Dan said loudly, "It's not a nice idea."

"I can see we're going to be at odds here. I'm a materialist, you see. An Epicurean, to be exact. And before you ask, it has nothing to do with the pleasures of the flesh."

"I don't know what you're on about," Dan said bluntly.

"You wouldn't be the only one," Mr Burton muttered ruefully. He cleared his throat, shifting giant quantities of phlegm. "At this moment I'm saying that a house is a simple arrangement of inanimate objects. It doesn't absorb emotions. No more than a tree can learn a poem. In the past Lowlake was an asylum, but the past is the past. Gone."

"I don't know. . ." I said uncertainly. "It's got . . . an atmosphere."

"If it does, you're the ones who are creating it. Such nonsense."

"You said yourself it was an unlucky house."

He laughed, a wet sound of mud and gravel being churned up on a river bed, and coughed quite disgustingly. He was able to splutter, "No, no, I said the people who lived there didn't have much luck. Quite different – and largely due to incompetence in all probability!"

"What do other people say about Lowlake?" Dan asked intelligently.

Mr Burton's cough began to subside. "Oh – *they'll* tell you it's an unlucky place. They think that's why it tends to stay empty and why, when people do move in, they move on again quite quickly. That's the peasant view. Primeval superstition – complete balderdash. But I'm afraid you've come to the wrong place if you're looking for foolish gossip!"

He leaned back and his eyes twinkled and he was again prey to a combination of coughing and laughing. "Not a reader among them! What am I doing here? Oh dear!"

I thought he was going to die, he laughed so much. It couldn't have been good for him.

At last he wiped his eyes, and his mouth, with his sleeve. "As a sceptic, knowledge and information are all I can give you. If you're still interested."

"We are," I said. "Tell us about the sanatorium."

He puffed on his cigarette and gave out what he knew concisely, along with gusts of recycled smoke. "At the start of the century, a Miss Armitage was the owner of Lowlake. Well-to-do spinster lady. When she died in the 1920s her will provided money for the house to be used for charitable purposes. The fact that Lowlake is miles from anywhere was why it became a home for the mentally ill. It could have been ideal, but there was always trouble in getting and keeping staff. Put it down to local ignorance and you wouldn't be too far out. The charitable bequest didn't last long and the place closed. There. Those are the plain facts."

They were. Very plain. I wouldn't give up, though. "You've got all these books. Is there anything about Lowlake in any of them?"

He ran through his entire stock in his mind – it appeared – then stubbed out his cigarette. "Wait there."

He went into the shop.

"Mandy."

"What, Dan?"

"He's not going to be any use, is he?"

"I don't think so, no."

"We just would get someone like him. He won't listen."

"He might if we could think of a good way to tell him," I suggested.

"He'd laugh. I hate it when he laughs."

"I think he might, yes."

"But what if John needs help?"

"Maybe we should try the doctor. I just don't know."

"He was a big-head."

"He's a *doctor*. He'd listen."

"Some doctors might – he wouldn't. He'd tell us to be brave little soldiers and not to be so silly. But there's something wrong with Lowlake. I know there is."

You don't know the half of it, I thought. *Unless I'm going mad. And I'm not.*

We sat there until Mr Burton bustled back in. He

carried an old magazine. "Sorry to keep you. I knew I had this somewhere."

"What is it?" I asked.

"Local journal. Do you want it?"

"What – to buy it?"

"Yes, well, that's what I do here – sell things. Five pounds and it's yours."

"Five pounds?" I said incredulously.

"Probably the only copy in existence. . ."

"I haven't got five pounds."

He smiled and coughed and gasped, "Have a look then, free . . . gratis. Centre spread. Sorry to tease."

He wasn't so bad. I took hold of the magazine and it fell open on the middle page. At the top it said, *"The High Peak Journal, June–August 1927"*. The headline read, *"Sanatorium Patients Take the Sunshine"* and the article started gaily, *"You could hardly find a more peaceful, happier spot. . ."*

Mr Burton was leaning over my shoulder, giving off tobacco odours all over me. I could hear his chest bubbling away inside as he remarked, "This was an attempt to allay local fears about having the sanatorium in the area. As you see. With all the ignorance and superstition around here I don't suppose for a moment that it worked."

There was a picture. Bizarre. It was of a game of croquet being played. It took me a moment to work out the exact setting. There was a tiny white temple there in the corner of the garden walls. . .

"There – do you see the Ice House?" Mr Burton said, close to my ear. "There's another example of nonsense for you. People began to say it was a bad place, where accidents happened. All arrant nonsense. They were ludicrously ill-informed. Knowledge is the only true power – did you know that? Sorry – I digress. The Ice House was built, very charmingly, as what we call a 'folly', an elegant little joke, but because it was designed like a temple the ignorant became fearful. It got a reputation and it was knocked down. Tragic."

So that was the Ice House. Not only had they knocked it down, but they had cut out that bit of garden all together. It must have been thought a very "bad place" if they went to those lengths.

I studied the rest of the picture. The croquet players and those watching seemed normal enough at first, until you realized that they all seemed to be looking in different directions and several held their heads at odd angles, as though not in full control of what they were doing.

In the foreground a woman in a long dress was lining up a shot through a hoop. The lawn wasn't really smooth enough for the game, I thought. Beside her was another woman, holding her mallet to her chest like it was something precious. And they were watched by the opposition: an elderly couple standing close together staring solemnly at the action. The caption read, "*Mrs Ethel Snell takes aim under the scrutiny of her playing partner and Mr and Mrs Jack Merriman.*"

Mr and Mrs Merriman were looking at the game in the fixed way they had looked at me when they stood behind Dan in the sitting room.

The bell sounded in the shop. Mr Burton ignored it. "It's still five pounds. I don't know why you should want it – but I have the instinct you do."

I answered very smartly – given my mental state just then – "I didn't know materialists allowed themselves instincts like that."

"Oh – ah-ha! Touché, young lady." Mr Burton's chest bubbled with pleasure – and John came into the room from the shop.

"Mandy – Dan. Come with me."

His eyes were wild; he was barely able to master his temper.

"We only—" I started.

"You only ran off without telling me where you were going! It won't do!"

"They seem responsible young people," Mr Burton said, surprised.

"They have no business running all over the countryside when I don't know where they are. It was lucky I saw the bikes outside."

Dan snapped back at him, just as angry as John was, "We weren't doing anything wrong."

"We have an arrangement. I have to know where

you are. Do you think it's easy bringing up two children by yourself?"

"Well, really, there's been no harm done," Mr Burton intervened again.

"How do I know? I know nothing about you. I want my children out of here right now."

"Not a very reasonable attitude," Mr Burton murmured. He seemed pleased to have his cynical view of his fellow man reinforced in this way.

John ignored him. "Out – out – out!" he commanded.

I gave the magazine to Mr Burton. "Thanks for your time."

"Oh I've got a lot of that."

John was physically propelling Dan from the room. He turned back to beckon to me imperiously.

"I'm sorry," I said sincerely to Mr Burton.

It made John madder than ever.

The drive back to Lowlake was not pleasant. John had thrown our bikes in the back of the Landrover without any consideration of the damage he might have done to them. With us he had been more restrained, I'm pleased to say.

He was driving flat out, with his foot right to the floor. A silence had come down on us all. I kept glancing at John's eyes in the driving mirror. Dan and I were in the back together. John's eyes didn't blink once. Stared straight down the road.

It was because I thought he might be slipping away from us again that I started to speak.

"We didn't have any arrangement," I said.

"Arrangement," he repeated blankly.

"About telling you where we were going."

"Amanda, it was an unspoken agreement, surely."

"No, it wasn't. Sorry – but it wasn't."

"It is too bad of you – truly. To be so disrespectful. I only have your welfare at heart."

He was speaking like an automaton, using strange, old-fashioned language. It was not nice. I could see Dan had noticed it too.

Dan said, "We didn't do anything wrong."

"It is a question of loyalty. Of *disloyalty* on your part. Good little children would never behave so. I regard it as a kind of betrayal."

"We don't like it at Lowlake," Dan went on doggedly.

"I do not wish to hear more on *that* subject, Daniel."

He had never used Dan's whole name before. He went on speaking. "The benefits of Lowlake are enormous. And – after consideration – I have decided you shall have ponies. If you wish."

"We don't want to be given anything more – that's not going to work!" My voice was rising in spite of my efforts to stay calm.

"All good young children have ponies. Be good and ponies you shall have."

"But—" I started.

"No more will be said on the subject of your absconding today. But it was hard of you – very hard – I swear it was. You have hurt me, children."

Oh boy. Could things get any worse, I wondered dully.

Well of course they could. A lot worse.

There was no food at all in the house. I caught John in the corridor before he could go back into his horrible room, and told him. He was terribly anxious to get back into the room and found it hard to speak to me.

Reaching far back for a very unimportant item in his memory he said, "I saw – yes . . . I've ordered some. There's money on the kitchen table to pay for it. . . More than enough, should I not be available."

"Sorry – what?"

"I rang a shop," he said impatiently, missing my point, "They deliver. They're going to deliver."

"Tonight?"

"I really don't know. Now I have to get back to my work. I'm sorry, Amanda, it's . . . it's – I have to go."

He opened the door without having to unlock it and slipped in before I could see inside. How about that. If only I had known he left the house without locking his room we could have worked a way to get a look inside. . . Now I heard him turning the key in the lock.

I went back into the kitchen and joined Dan. Even in here I felt trapped. On the table was a little heap of banknotes, but the shops in Essop would be shut now. No one would be delivering food at this time of day.

There on the wall was the speaking tube. I shuddered. I didn't even want to go near it. But above all else, I didn't want to go back upstairs.

"We've got to get something done about this, Mandy," Dan said. He sat at the table with his head in his hands. All his natural energy had left him.

"There'll be some food coming in the morning," I said.

His head jerked up. "I don't mean food!" I saw there were tears in his eyes.

"No, I didn't suppose you did," I said hopelessly.

Apathetically, he began to finger the money on the table, pushing it around.

"Don't do that," I said. I collected the notes and counted them. John had left far too much: there was over fifty pounds here. I put it in my back pocket and, immediately, the possession of money boosted my confidence, as it so often does.

My eye caught the telephone on the Welsh dresser. I strode towards it. "We'll have to. Have to phone Gran. What else can we do."

I didn't know the number of the nursing home but, with the decision taken, nothing was going to

115

stop me. I dialled Directory Enquiries and they answered immediately.

"Hello?" The woman said on the crackly line.

"Yes," I said. "I need a Manchester number."

"I'm sure we can help you, dear."

"Yes – it's the number of –"

The woman interrupted, "We really would like to help you."

She sounded rather old to be a telephone operator. I said, "It's a nursing home called—"

And the old man's voice breathed down the telephone line, "Or would you like to help *us*?"

I dropped the phone as if it was red hot. Dan was staring at me. We both looked at the telephone receiver twisting on its cord as it dangled to the ground and we both heard the laughter cackling out of the instrument.

"Oh no," Dan said.

There was a splitting sound and the wire of the telephone shot out of the skirting board, breaking the connection, and there was silence for a second before the whole dresser started to shake as though someone was heaving at it. Cups and plates fell to the stone floor and broke.

I turned to Dan. "Out," I said. "Get out."

The calendar fell down from the wall: the picture hanger had popped right out. With a terrible scraping sound the kitchen table began to turn itself around and around on the spot.

The light bulb in the ceiling exploded sharply, showering us with fine glass as we ran out of the room.

I slammed the door shut. Behind us we heard the carnage increasing in the kitchen. Dan was whimpering with fear.

In the hall we hesitated, literally not knowing which way to turn, unco-ordinated by panic. There was a great, complicated crash as the whole of the dresser was thrown to the floor.

We ran. Along the corridor and into the open part of the hall where the stairs began. I dragged Dan to the front door and wrestled with the handle. It wouldn't turn. The door was sealed shut. I began to make little noises of fear too.

We heard the kitchen door being dragged open, carrying broken crockery with it. An elderly voice called in a sprightly fashion, "Coming! Ready or not!"

We ran for the stairs and the running footsteps came after us.

10

The next moments were terrifying beyond belief. At the top of the stairs I turned to look back and saw that at the bottom the air was distorted by two transparent writhing shapes. It was as if these inexplicit apparitions were made of a heavier air that was shot through with colours like oil on water. You couldn't say they were the shapes of people, they were too fluid and indistinct.

The wriggling masses of air came up the stairs with a glutinous licking sound. I screamed and ran after Dan. Oh no! He was going straight for our sitting room. Behind us the chilling noises had disappeared. . .

I accelerated but could not catch him before he opened the door and flung himself in. "No – Dan!"

There they were, the Merrimans, side by side, ethereal, immobile, smiling and smiling.

"Get *out*!" I bawled, grabbing Dan. And then I realized that he was looking right at the insubstantial forms of the old people and could not see them.

Mr and Mrs Merriman seemed to gaze at me affectionately, acknowledging that I was the only one to whom they were visible. Was it my imagination – or did their smiles get broader?

I pulled Dan out of the room using brute strength and shut the door again.

"Not in *there*," I told him.

"Where then? We've got to get out of here, Mandy," he whispered in terror.

"Yes – the back door!" I gasped, and together we sprinted back to the stairs. That hideous licking noise started up again, chasing us – and extremely fast. How we got down the stairs without falling I don't know. We dashed along to the kitchen to get to the back door and there in front of us was one of the sinuous shapes in the air, coiling and squirming. A voice came from it, that of an old man: "*You are ours, to do with as we please.*"

"Oh!" Dan cried out, but though he could hear well enough I was sure he still didn't see anything.

We turned. At the other end of the passage was another of the oily distortions in the air.

"Ours for ever," the old woman's voice called.

Dan began shouting, "John! John!" at the top of his voice.

It was no use at all. The swirling air shapes started to close in on us, speaking. The man said "We are your masters." His voice was getting deeper and stronger, a rolling bass.

The woman's voice was getting higher and wilder, "Your deserts are durance vile!"

"Or death," the man intoned.

We were shuffling to a position equidistant from both apparitions. It was the best we could do.

Dan screamed again, "John! John!"

The man boomed, "Surrender!"

"Or die!" The woman shrieked.

"Or die," the man rumbled.

The shapes progressed towards us inexorably. Having seen what had happened in the kitchen I had no doubts that they could harm us, but I was curiously calm now. Beside us was the door to the drawing room and just ahead the door to the one little room we had never decorated: the damp one that was going to be used for boots and umbrellas. I tugged the resisting Dan down the hall towards it.

"In there," I said and opened the door. The shapes gathered themselves and surged towards us as I dragged Dan in and slammed the door.

There was a sticky sound as something hurled itself against the door with an impact that shook it. And then silence.

"Oh Mandy. . ." Dan said, and we held on to each other.

Something began tapping at the door.

"You mustn't go in there," the old woman's voice came earnestly.

"It is forbidden," the old man's voice breathed.

"Death will come a'calling while you sleep," the woman assured us with scratchy glee.

"It matters not how good you are now. You will not escape punishment," said the man.

"You have been naughty," the woman said coyly. "That is the forbidden room and you will be punished. There are rules. . ."

They started to speak one after the other with no pause in between.

"Say your prayers every night." the man called sadly.

"Wash behind your ears."

"Eat what is on your plate."

"Wipe your boots when you come in from the wet."

"Wipe your nose when you have a cold."

"And *never* look in your handkerchief afterwards."

I butted in on them. I said steadily, "Who are you?"

"We are your betters," the voices came in unison, "You are nothing."

"Who are you?" I repeated very clearly.

There was a pause.

The woman said coldly, "We are disappointed in you."

You could hear that disappointment in the heavy silence that fell. Then I had the impression that gradually the silence was getting lighter, as though they were moving away. . .

Dan and I waited, gripping each other less tightly with each passing moment. No more voices came.

"They can't get in here," Dan whispered. "How did you know?"

"Luck, I suppose."

"It's ghosts. Real ghosts. Of mad people."

"You can't see them, can you?"

"What – you mean you can?"

"Sometimes. A bit," I said carefully.

"Who are they?"

Exhausted, I shrugged. Excitement at that level drains you very quickly.

Outside it began to rain; one of those sudden, continuous downpours that can stop as quickly as they start.

There was a speaking tube on the wall. I took my shoes off and Dan watched and did not comment as I removed my socks to use them as wadding to seal the mouthpiece of the tube. Whether or not this would be effective I didn't know, but I had the unsettling notion that if I didn't do something we would be listened to through it.

I looked around the sad little room. Well, at least it wasn't too cold. We'd probably get rheumatism or something, though. . .

I lay down on the wooden floorboards.

"What are you doing," Dan said, appalled.

"I'm going to get some sleep."

"How could you?"

"I need to sleep, so I'm going to. I can't think straight like I am now."

"What about me?"

"Just don't go out of here and you'll be OK. Probably."

I was yawning. Dan came to sit down right next to me so we were touching again.

"You're selfish," he said. "I hate you."

I tried to make a pillow with my arms. "No you don't."

Sleep didn't come for ages, though I pretended to Dan that it had, keeping my eyes shut. Behind them all sorts of random thoughts and memories darted around in my mind. None of them made any sense, but I guessed this was my subconscious beginning to process information. . . Sorting through it all. . .

The busy thoughts must have become dreams at some point because all of a sudden I was waking up. It was pitch dark. I could feel Dan curled into me like a faithful dog.

The silence. Not threatening. Me lying there, the floorboards twice as hard as they had been. So very dark. . . Me not thinking any more, just being a living, breathing creature.

Me falling asleep again.

The front door bell.

It was daylight.

"What?" Dan mumbled.

There were no curtains in the dank little room. I looked out of the window. It was misty, but I could see that a nondescript van stood by the Landrover.

"You stay where you are," I told Dan, "I'll go."

"Where?"

"Someone's at the front door."

He struggled up. "No – no – don't leave me."

"You're safe here."

"If you're going, I'm coming."

It was no fun venturing into the hall, but nothing peculiar happened. We went quickly to the front door. I wondered if we were still trapped inside Lowlake. . .

However, the door opened as usual. A fat young man stood there holding a big cardboard box. It looked heavy.

"Oh," he said, disappointed. "Your dad in?"

"Yes," Dan said at the same moment that I said, "No."

"Delivery. I can't leave this without getting

paid," the young man said, going red with embarrassment.

"What is it?"

"It's the food, Mandy," Dan giggled stupidly.

"Yes of course," I said coolly. "So – how much is it?"

"Twenty one pound fifty-nine," the young man said, with no hope of getting his money.

"Right." I took out the wad of notes from my back pocket and peeled off two tens and a five pound note. "Keep the change."

It was my turn to blush after I said that. It didn't sound terribly sophisticated coming from a teenager.

The young man said, "Where d'you want it?"

"Oh, just leave it there."

He set the box down. "Everything all right?"

"Fine." Something in our manner must have troubled him. He lingered.

"So, where's your Dad?"

"Asleep. He gave me the money because he didn't want to be disturbed."

"Oh. Well . . . I'll be off."

"OK. Bye. And thanks."

We watched him walking to his van, getting in . . . and all at once Dan began to talk very fast.

"Get him back, Mandy! The van – we could get John out of here – with that bloke's help! Don't just let him go!"

"Yes – Dan – brilliant – you're right!"

We stepped out of Lowlake as the young man started his van. Over the noise of the engine there came a sharp disturbance of the air and there was a splintering thud right beside my neck.

Sticking deep into the door frame was a metal object with three small fins on its tail.

"We can't, Dan." I said as tranquilly as I could. "They won't let us."

Dan saw where I was pointing. I felt a warm trickle on my collar-bone: a thin rivulet of blood was running down my neck. Near miss? Warning? Or didn't they care? Feeling sick, I returned the young man's wave as he swung the van around and motored away from the house.

Dan was tugging at the metal object embedded in the door-frame. He couldn't get it out. "It's one of my bolts!" he said, amazed, "From my crossbow!"

"Yes," I said.

"You're bleeding!"

"It's all right. Honestly."

He stood back and I felt the crossbow bolt. It was slightly gritty to the touch, just starting to rust. It was the one Dan had lost in the garden.

"There's five more of those somewhere, Mandy," Dan said, scared.

"They won't use them if we behave ourselves." I hoped.

I bent down and opened the cardboard box. It was stacked to the top with cans. Baked beans, peas, baked beans, more baked beans, and . . . lots more baked beans.

"What's the point of all the baked beans?" Dan queried.

"He didn't have his mind on it when he made the phone call."

"It's like he's not John any more. I miss him. I was getting used to him. I liked him."

"I like him too."

"Can't we all leave? We could somehow, couldn't we?"

"I don't think we can."

"But what do they want?"

I couldn't answer him.

From inside the house an unexpected sound made itself heard.

Music.

A woman began to sing, "Love's Old Sweet Song".

"*Once in the dear dead days beyond recall,*" the voice warbled melodiously, "*When on the world the mists began to fall. . .*"

Of course it was a recording, but there was something very eerie about hearing such an old song coming from the house.

"I think we're being invited to something," I said. The chill I felt made its way into my voice.

"Don't let's go."

I gave him a look and turned my back on the daylight and went inside.

He came after me. The music was coming from John's room. We walked down the dark corridor, under the pictures of the ships at sea which hung on the walls with the grandiose landscapes . . . and with the sound of the old song getting louder all the while.

"Just a song at twilight, when the lights are low, and the flick'ring shadows softly come and go. . ."

The door was shut.

"We can't get in. That's that," Dan said with relief.

Too soon.

Slowly, the door opened.

We stepped into the past.

11

John was sitting in the chair, unseeing. He wore a dark old-fashioned suit with small lapels on the jacket, and a shirt with a high shiny collar. The music was coming from the wind-up gramophone with its massive flower-bell trumpet that acted as an amplifier.

"Even today we hear Love's song of yore . . . deep in our hearts it dwells for evermore. . ."

The shutters were shut and the heavy brocade curtains too, and a whole world had been re-created in here. Two tall standard lamps with red shades lit the semi-gloom. The room was grand and immaculate and there were reflections everywhere: from the massive mirror above the fireplace; from the heavy, shiny mahogany furniture; from the polished glass case where the dead ducks were imprisoned.

The music played on, getting slower and less tuneful as the clockwork mechanism ran down. *"Still to the end when life's dim shadows fall"*, the singer slurred deeper and deeper, her voice becoming masculine and out of tune.

The wind-up handle on the gramophone began turning fast all by itself and the singer perked up, getting back into her stride.

The door swung shut behind us. That did it. Oblivious to danger, on the verge of tears, Dan marched forward and took hold of John's shoulders.

"Wake up! Wake up, John! Please!"

John stared straight ahead, quite unaware of our presence in the room. He looked like the man in the picture we found under the Ice House. Very like him, now.

I walked slowly to the gramophone. The handle revolved itself more quickly and the woman began to sing faster than she ought to. *"Though the heart be weary, sad the day and long, still to us at twilight comes Love's old song!"*

The needle of the gramophone was contained in a round sort of thing on an arm. I swept the arm from the record and a destructive, scratching sound screeched from the big horn-amplifier. And there was quiet.

"That's enough." I called. My voice broke into a sob. "*Enough*. What do you want?"

Silence. A silence of consideration.

The two lights went out. The darkness was like that of late evening.

"Hello again," the old woman's voice said brightly.

"Hello," I replied as conversationally as I could. Shaking all over, I walked to where Dan stood by John. Looked around very deliberately. Where were they?

There was a series of short sniggers from the old woman. I couldn't see them, couldn't even tell where her voice came from. When the man spoke the booming bass came from somewhere up near the ceiling.

"We don't want you."

"We have what we want," the old woman cackled – it was a definite cackle. Their characters had developed into witch and warlock, it seemed to me. I couldn't imagine that Mr and Mrs Merriman had spoken that way.

"You have our father, yes," I said. My mouth was dry with fear. "What are you going to do with him?"

Dan said, "We want him back!"

I told him, "Leave this to me." I raised my voice. "I want an answer!"

There was a turbulence in the atmosphere. Over in the corner furthest from the window. I had the impression some kind of conference was taking place – some kind of dialogue between the spirits, or whatever they were.

The old woman spoke again, sounding plaintive, "He can't see us."

And they were off again, taking turns to speak and sometimes chiming in together. Their voices were much more normal this time.

The old man breathed, "You have the gift, but he has not."

"He must be able to see us," the old woman whined.

"There is one way only."

Together: "He must be as we are. He must join us."

Dan whispered, horrified, "They're going to kill him – kill John."

The old man answered him. "We would not do that. He will die, that is all, and in a matter of days he will be with us wholly."

"He is fading as you watch him," the old woman said softly, "He does not eat, so the outcome is inevitable."

"He will slip away so peacefully. We are gentle with him. We are good."

"We are good. He will be with us."

They said as one, "We will be together."

Not if I can help it, I thought. "And us – what about us?" I called out.

"We don't want you." they said, and you could hear the indifference in their voices, "Live your lives. Live them somewhere else."

The man said, "Or stay. It's all one to us."

The woman was a witch again as she screamed, "But bring any other grown-up man or woman here and all will die: you are warned – all will perish horribly!"

The man said in a sinister, confidential tone, "We can do it, you know."

The curtains shifted as a wind got up inside the room. The voices moved around the room restlessly. "Decide. We must have your answer. Decide!"

I bent over John. He was breathing, but very shallowly. He felt cold to the touch.

"We need your answer. Now he is ours, beyond your interference, we must know how it is to be. Do you stay? Or do you go?"

"Why not take us too?" I shouted defiantly.

The voices were icy. "Never."

"Give us time," I pleaded. "We have to think about what's best. Give us time."

The bass voice came back at its most impressive. "By tomorrow. He will not be long in your world."

"He will be with us within days," the woman hissed.

"Give us your answer by tomorrow night," the man growled. "Before the clock strikes twelve. Bring no one here, tell no one, or all will perish."

"We can't leave him," Dan said to me, with agony on his face.

The lights sprang back into life. Suspended in the air in front of us was the crossbow with a bolt at the ready.

"Come on, Dan," I took hold of him and we blundered out of the room.

The door crashed itself shut behind us.

In there John was slipping away from us by gentle degrees and I didn't know what we could do about it.

We went back to "the forbidden room" where we had spent the night. My guess was that not only were we safe in here, but that the spirits could not or would not listen in to us either.

Dan was in a state and of course I was too, but I knew one of us had to think clearly, because there was no one but us who could do anything. The whole world was out there, in the bland light of day, beyond the walls of Lowlake, but we might as well have been on a crewless ship in the middle of a vast ocean. If I want to remember how it feels to be lonely, I remember that morning.

"I think it takes a long time to die just because you're not eating," I said, trying to find something positive in our situation.

"They're not reasonable!" Dan protested wildly, "They're crazy! How do they think we could go on living here by ourselves? That money wouldn't last – people would come – and there would be John, dead. . ."

He blinked hard and swallowed. I tried to think it through. "And what would we tell those people, if they did come? You know what would happen? We'd be the ones who got put in a loony bin."

And suddenly it all fell into place. They weren't mad people at all. They were something else.

"Listen to me, Dan – they've got him done up like that picture – he looks like the picture – right? That's going way, way back. . ." It was coming to me in a rush, all at once. "This isn't anything to do with the sanatorium. What about that list of rules they came up with last night? 'Don't look in your handkerchief', for heaven's sake! And that was a little shrine we found under the Ice House. It was in memory of this man who looks like John – long before Lowlake became an asylum!"

Dan only looked blank. I gave him my idea anyway.

"They're children, Dan."

Now he was dumbfounded. "No. No, Mandy. They're old."

I was almost laughing with excitement as the thoughts kept tumbling out. "Don't you see? They can put on any voices they want to! All right, so I've seen them – but it's all a trick – they looked like a couple from the asylum but they just stood there –

it was fake – like some kind of projection. And what about that stuff about them being 'good' – and about us not bringing in any *grown-ups*? I'm right, Dan!"

He couldn't take it in and that made him angry. "Fine – fine," he shouted, "But even if it's all true – how exactly does it help us!"

"Well there's another thing I've remembered. Something Mr Burton told us. He said, 'Knowledge is power'. If we want to *do* anything we need more information. We didn't take him back far enough because we were only interested in the asylum. We've got to go to him again."

"All that way? We haven't got time!" Dan despaired.

I got steely. "Well do tell me if you've anything better to do."

"And you think they'll let us just go off somewhere – just like that?"

He might be being negative but he had a point there. In the end we agreed that the ghosts had, after all, offered us the chance to leave, although to go and get the bikes could attract unwelcome attention. We would have to sneak out of the window in this room and get back in the same way.

If we could.

The weather was on our side at this stage. The day was cool and damp and the morning mist had thickened. It was hard to open the window: long exposure to the moist air had swollen the wooden frame. It was hard, too, to climb out, in the knowledge that at any moment a crossbow bolt could come zinging at you. . .

We wanted to run, but I had told Dan that we had to stroll away as if we felt quite secure in what we were doing. The urge to go faster made me get a pain in my stomach. The mist was thick enough to keep visibility low: I could see details of the landscape only within a twenty metre radius. It made it much worse, giving you not so much the fear but the almost certain *knowledge* that someone or something was going to jump out at you.

But there was no jumping out. No high-velocity crossbow bolts. Only the pounding of our living hearts.

Oh, but the time it took just to get out of that misty hollow. . . Time, precious time. . . Dan looked at it ticking away on his watch. "It's going to take so long," he moaned and, as one, we began to jog.

"Ammunition," I panted at last when we could no longer see any trace of the house. "That's what we need. Weapons to fight them with."

"I can't keep this up, Mandy."

"Don't think about it. Think about what we know and what we can *do*."

We jogged on, thinking so furiously that we couldn't think at all. It took us three quarters of an hour to reach the road, by the signpost showing

"Lowlake", and despite ourselves we had slowed to a fast walk.

As we hit the tarmac of the narrow road Dan said breathessly, "John knew. Even if he didn't know he knew."

"Sorry?"

"Our sitting room. Don't you remember? He called it the nursery when he said we were going to have it for our own place."

"He did, didn't he!"

"How would he know that?"

"You're right, Dan. And what about all those old-fashioned things he got us – things for old-fashioned kids?"

"That's true, too!" He was getting enthusiastic about the idea now. There's nothing like making your own original contribution to make you feel involved. "And, Mandy. . ."

"Yes?"

"You forgot about the letter. The one we nearly burnt. It didn't have to have been written to loonies. It could just as well have been written to children. Actually, that's much more likely. Don't you think?"

"Yes. . . Yes!" I tried to remember its contents. John had so quickly snaffled everything we had found.

"*My dear ones. . .*" Something about them feeling like prisoners. Why?

I said, "There was a ship, wasn't there. . ."

"With a name like 'water', yes."

"It was going to Africa. John got the name wrong at first. The *Wanderer*, the *Wanter* . . . the *Wanton*. . ."

But we couldn't remember the name of the ship. And would it help, even if we did?

We marched on with legs that got heavier and heavier and I was more and more depressed. We were walking directly away from our father, on a fool's mission more than likely.

12

As we came down into Essop we saw cars and bikes and people going about their business as normal. But there was never any question in my mind that we were going to tell anyone about our problems. The people we saw were cut off from us by the threat to John's life. And to ours, too.

It would have been lunchtime or thereabouts. I was surprised to find I was getting hungry, and I felt guilty that in these circumstances I could even think about food.

Life goes on.

"He'd better be there," Dan said in sudden consternation.

"He will be," I said confidently.

As we got close to the bookshop we saw that the sign said SHUT.

My empty stomach turned a somersault. Something bitter came up into the back of my throat.

"It doesn't mean he isn't there. I'm going to knock."

I did. Knocked and waited.

Knocked and waited. And waited.

The plan, such as it was, had failed before it had even begun. Standing here in Essop, with passers-by staring at us, it seemed to have been a very fragile plan in the first place.

"This is terrible," Dan said in a small voice. "We've come all this way. Miles away from John."

All this way, for nothing? No. "Come on – we're not giving up. There was that magazine . . . there might be other stuff in there. We'll break in."

"We can't do that!"

"Got to," I said simply. "Because I can't think of anything else to do."

A dirt lane served the yards and gardens at the back of the buildings and right next to Mr Burton's premises a door was wide open, revealing a little timber yard. We crept in, alert and criminal, and saw no one. Within seconds we pushed a packing case to the wooden fence and clambered over, feeling momentarily conspicuous at the top – and dropped down into Mr Burton's garden, which was weedy enough to be declared a nature reserve.

"Break in how?" Dan muttered.

I didn't answer. Went up and pressed my face against the grimy glass of the back window.

Just as Mr Burton came into the tiny kitchen carrying a mug.

"Hey!" he shouted hoarsely.

"Run!" Dan called.

"Why?" I said. And stood my ground.

The back door opened. "What's the meaning—" Mr Burton croaked, and then he recognized me. "Oh. It's you."

"Yes."

"Persistent little tykes, aren't you?"

"Yes. We hadn't finished speaking to you."

He looked around. "Where's your father?"

"He won't bother us this time. Why are you shut? Why didn't you answer your bell?"

"It wouldn't worry me if he did turn up again. I don't appreciate being browbeaten." But he looked around again anyway. Next, he took in our dishevelled state. "So. Been out in the fresh air having –" he seemed to search for the word – "fun? That's good. . . Come on in."

"Really?" My delight was plain to hear.

"Yes, really. And count yourselves lucky. I'm taking the day off. Seem to have picked up some kind of chest infection."

He did look quite ghastly. We went in after him, back to his private room.

It was not a place for someone with a chest condition. The sweet, liverish smell of tobacco was stronger than ever and another butt burned in the ashtray.

"Tea?" Mr Burton gasped. "I was just getting another cup."

"Well – all right."

He shuffled off so slowly I wanted to take a cattle prod to him. When the tea came it was a dark metallic brew that could have been boiled up from industrial waste. We were thirsty enough to sip at it and make appreciative noises.

"What are you after, exactly?" Mr Burton asked, with shrewd eyes gazing over the rim of his steaming cup. The hot drink had eased his discomfort for the moment.

"Same thing. We want to know about Lowlake."

"Want to tell me why?"

"Um – no. I mean – it's our home. We're interested."

"Looking for stories so you can scare yourself to sleep?"

"No – we don't need any, thanks," Dan said with simple truth.

"And we've got money this time," I added quickly.

"Have you? Jolly good. I could certainly do with some. Expensive habit, smoking."

I didn't have time to get into the complexities of

his addiction. "I think what we'd like to hear about is what Lowlake was like before it was a mental institution. Say, sometime around the start of this century."

"I don't follow. It was just as it is now. Actually – very much like it is now."

Something had occurred to Mr Burton and to our horror he began to laugh again. It was a dry, hacking noise today, with the occasional explosion of phlegm coming from deep down, like molten lava threatening an eruption from the bottom of a volcano.

"That's better! Thank you," he said surprisingly as he wiped his mouth.

"What did you mean?" I asked, "Very much like it is now?"

"Yes – well – after all the mining and the farming it became a private house when this Miss Armitage bought it. I told you about her."

"Not much."

"No? Well, there was a Mr and Mrs Judd. . ."

Mr Burton's method of story-telling was all too comprehensive. In order to tell us about Miss Armitage he went back to the previous owners, a childless couple who had run the farm into the ground. Finally he got back to where we wanted him.

"The Judds sold up before the First World War. I think he volunteered for that show – though he was much too old – and got shot dead, of course, for his pains. . . I don't think theirs was a happy marriage. . . Anyway, the new owner was our Miss Armitage. A sour sort of person, one imagines – a selfish type – who wanted nothing better than to be left alone by one and all. . . A misanthropist, in short, to whom the isolation of Lowlake was its chief appeal. . . In some ways you could say that hers was the unhappiest tenure of all. . . I heard of this from my own father, though the details have been somewhat obscured by time. . ."

"In short," had he said? If only he would be!

But we were getting to it now.

"Now then," Mr Burton said, putting down his tea, getting into his stride, "There she is, stuck up there, content with her own company, when out of the blue comes her brother. John."

John.

"John?"

"Yes. Her younger brother. They had both been left very well provided for – it had been a rich family – but in retrospect he seems to have been just the kind of unfortunate individual Lowlake seems to attract. . . Like Miss Armitage herself. . . It really is quite an extraordinary tale. . ."

So tell it, I urged silently.

He coughed some more and drank some more tea and inhaled deeply on his latest cigarette. His voice grew stronger.

"Yes – Miss Armitage's brother. As I understand it he was an energetic, appealing man who had married a very pretty wife but had no business sense. And no luck, either, if one wants to speak of that commodity. . . Not only did his wife die at a very early age, but he lost all his money too. I understand he spent several years at Lowlake, attempting to make a go of the farm again, before he sailed for Australia to try his hand at yet another farming enterprise – leaving the children with his sister."

"Sorry – what?" I said sharply. "Children?"

"Yes. Didn't I mention the children?"

"No," Dan said.

"Oh yes – I must have – because that's why I said it was just as it is now – with two children there and only one adult. You see?"

"What were they like – the children?" I asked eagerly.

"I've no idea," Mr Burton said blankly. "They were just children."

"How old?"

"I don't know. It was a boy and a girl and they were . . . children." He excused his lack of knowledge about them by adding, "They weren't there very long."

"Oh," I said, disappointed. "They moved?"

"No. They died."

13

I knew Dan had looked at me sharply but I kept my eyes on Mr Burton and assumed a bland expression.

"Oh dear," I said lightly.

"Oh, sad, yes. And much worse than that, quite unnecessary."

"How do you mean?"

"I mean one would have to blame Miss Armitage. She was extremely unhappy about the children being left with her – and the result was that she rather let them run wild. One night she came down here to raise a search party. They had gone missing. Died on the High Peak somewhere. . . Down an old mine shaft? I mustn't speculate, must I. Their bodies were never found. No one was enormously shocked – these things happen round here if you don't know what you're doing. But it was sad. They vanished shortly before their father was to come back, after his latest venture had gone the way of all the others he'd tried. I think it's safe to say that Miss Armitage was desperately guilty about the children, but they had been seen playing well over a mile from the house on more than one occasion, so their disappearance was hardly a million to one chance."

"What were their names?" I asked.

"Oh I don't know that."

"Miss Armitage doesn't come out of it too well," I said.

Mr Burton agreed with a sad shake of his head. "Perhaps that was why she stipulated that her estate would be used for charitable purposes. The remorse, you know. She went a bit quaint, up there all alone, and some twelve years later she died herself – in tragic circumstances. Or comic ones, some might say."

"Comic?"

"She drowned in just a few inches of water that had surfaced in the famous lake. There was talk of suicide, but – well – who knows. . ."

He stubbed out his cigarette and lit another one. As he shook the match to make it go out he said with beaming sincerity, "Well – this is splendid, isn't it! I'm so glad you called. I feel so much better."

And he coughed uproariously. The lava was more liquid now and shifted about in his lungs.

Dan studied him with distaste. "And Mr Armitage?" he asked, "Her brother? What happened to him?"

Annoyed not to get in first with this vital question, I took over. "Was he killed in the First World World too? Like Mr Judd?"

Mr Burton leaned forward energetically, inserting himself into a cloud of smoke he had just released. "No no. What happened to Mr Armitage is a story in itself. . . He was lost at sea, somewhere off the coast of Africa."

"How extraordinary," I enthused, "How did that come about? And – um – when?"

From the sudden energy he had displayed I was prepared for another long tale – and this time I looked forward to it.

But he said without interest, "Nineteen-ten? Somewhere around then. Now, I'm feeling well enough to open for business, so. . ."

"But what about Mr Armitage?"

"What about him? He went down in an ocean liner and that was the end of him."

"But—"

"I've told you the entire history of Lowlake – what more do you want? I don't know anything more about it. You know as much as I do now."

He was getting to his feet. I got up too.

"Oh – but – what about books then? Have you got anything more about Lowlake? In a book?"

He was already on his way to his shop, trailing plumes of smoke.

"No. There aren't any. Why would there be?"

We were out on the main street again before we knew it, hustled out by Mr Burton, who had had enough of the company of young people.

"They want John for their dad," Dan said in disbelief.

"Their dad – John."

"But he's *our* dad!"

Walking aimlessly, we went over what we now knew – and couldn't for the life of us see how it might be used to our advantage. It seemed unarguable that the ghosts were in the process of appropriating our father to take the place of the one they had lost, but as to what we could do about it. . .

I found myself repeating, "I'm not going to be beaten by a couple of kids."

"We've got to get back, Mandy."

"There's no point – until we've got a plan. I'll tell you one thing – I'm going to give them a good talking-to."

'Yes? And that's the plan? That's going to make them give up, is it? They'll kill us," Dan said bleakly. "One way or another. All they want is John,

150

and they've got him. We're just in the way as far as they're concerned."

"We've got that room. The forbidden one. They don't go in there."

"Yes – and you're going to give them a talking-to," he said sarcastically, "So what else do we need?"

Just for an instant I found myself thinking, *I wish we had another parent. There's no one we can even talk to.*

And almost at once Dan was saying, "Other people are lucky. They've got a mum as well as a dad."

And just after that I said, "I'm going back to the bookshop," and Dan said, "I've got an idea, actually. Can I have some of the money?"

Moments later we split up. Had we somehow received help from somewhere? I'll never know and at that moment I didn't much care. Just as I didn't care if Mr Burton was going to be testy with me – there would be something more amongst his stock and I was going to find it. I don't know how I was so positive, but I was. Dan hadn't told me his idea and I hadn't asked about it – I was concentrating everything on "knowledge is power".

Back at the shop, Mr Burton was too nice to say he was fed up with me – but he was. He sat at his little desk and I started on his stock.

Encyclopedias were no help. Local books,

however old, were useless. History books only told you about battles and laws and important historical figures. I was looking for stuff on Lowlake and some more on Mr Armitage's sunken ship – John Armitage's watery grave. . .

Through the window I saw Dan come back with a carrier bag. He grimaced at me through the glass, looking somehow shamefaced and not very confident about whatever it was he had been doing, and stayed in the street. He would be impatient with me, but I wouldn't go yet even if I had to examine the contents of every book in the shop. By now Mr Burton must have begun to believe I was one of the fixtures and fittings.

Dan had gone again. I searched on.

It was in one of the piles of books on the floor: that was why it took so long to find it. *Great Maritime Misadventures*. The glossy leather of the cover had turned to brown suede and the spine was coming away, but on page 352 there it was.

"1908, July 27th, THE WARATAH, *9,339 tons, quadruple expansion engines, Blue Anchor Line. Lost at sea and never found."*

I took it over to the desk. "Can I buy this?"

Mr Burton was reading a book in Latin. "*The Twelve Caesars*", he said, holding it up before he laid it down. "Reads like a modern novel! You couldn't have a more lively account. Now then, let me see. . ."

The sea-disasters book cost fifteen pounds, which Mr Burton said was cheap, "Since it's been that price since I got it – years ago."

It didn't seem so cheap to me but I took it. I bought, too, the journal with the article about Lowlake, just in case it could be useful, although I knew I was clutching at straws there.

Dan had not gone anywhere; he was sitting outside the shop below window-level with his carrier bag between his feet.

"You've been ages."

"I know what happened to the father."

"Oh. . ."

"What did you get?"

He was embarrassed. "Oh. Nothing. Nothing useful, I don't suppose. It seemed like a good idea when I thought of it."

I told Dan, "It's like a battle. We've got to be good and ready for it," and so we took more of the precious time to talk through what we'd got, sitting like beggars outside The Copper Pot, where lucky tourists guzzled sugar and starch under dark wooden beams that were actually made of plaster. It was ironic: we had enough money for the best meal Essop had to offer and we couldn't bring ourselves to eat a thing while our father sat comatose in Lowlake.

It was already late afternoon and the weather was

turning sultry. I read out to Dan the passage about the *Waratah*. He agreed it must be the ship referred to in the letter from the trunk.

She was bound from Australia to England, going by way of the Cape. At Durban, in Africa, one passenger had abandoned the ship, expressing doubts about her sea-worthiness. He had noticed that she took a long time to get upright again when she rolled in heavy seas. Her next stop was Cape Town. She never arrived. No trace of the *Waratah* was ever found, nor of the two hundred and eleven persons on board.

Dan said, "I had that dream about Africa. . ."

"I had my own dream too, about the father going away. That's what it was. I didn't know then, but now I'm sure that was it."

I wanted to know what Dan had in his carrier bag. He was reluctant to show me. "It's silly."

I took it from him and went through the things he had bought. He described his idea to me and when I made the mistake of agreeing that it was silly he got stubborn.

"It might work. You never know. At least I came up with a plan, which is more than you have."

It was time to go. We had spent hours and hours away from Lowlake.

The road out of Essop was mostly uphill. A young couple in Bermuda shorts were striding up it. The man had an underfed beard and a nasal voice and he said cheerfully, "Going our way? Want some company?"

I said flatly, "No."

If it had been scary leaving Lowlake, it was a lot worse going back after a break from it. The fear we felt was like a third person with us who kept us silent the whole, long journey.

It was strangely hard to breathe on the last half-mile, up on the high moorland. The sun was low and swollen in the sky and the air was charged with static. It looked like we could have a storm.

"We've been away so long," Dan panted.

My legs ached so much. I saved my breath and didn't answer him. Unconsciously we were walking faster. Hurrying now. . .

A great white light ruptured the sky. The long low rumble of thunder was deep and distant.

More sheet lightning illuminated the countryside, bleaching the colour from our surroundings, turning the grass to an unearthly iridescent lime colour.

When I glanced at him Dan himself looked like a ghost. Pale and insubstantial. And frightened.

I read his mind. "It's nature, Dan. They can't organize something on this scale."

The storm continued, dry like Mr Burton's cough had been, with the thunder and lightning tearing and ripping at the sky as if crazy with pain and wanting to split it open and release the rain.

There below was Lowlake. Another distress-flare of lightning showed the old house at its worst, stark and forbidding. Then the rain finally hit us like a wave falling from deep space and we glanced at each other, took in a deep breath and began to run.

Perhaps all the rain and the electricity in the air interfered with the ghosts' powers of perception, or perhaps they were obessessed with John, or perhaps they just never thought we would return, because I had the instinct as we ran the last metres that we were going to make it. Dan was a little way behind me. He called, "My matches are going to be useless."

"Keep your voice down."

We were soaked to the bone by the time we got back to the window we had climbed out of those hours ago. Scrabbling with my fingernails I pulled it open and threw in the stuff we had bought, shoved Dan through, and followed.

We were back in the dank, dim room. I forced the window shut again. Outside the storm battered at the house and rattled everything it could.

Dan laid out his purchases on the floor. Two lemons. A pad of writing paper. A box of matches. Some candles. A wooden dip-pen with a thick nib. An egg cup and several reels of cotton, of different colours.

"I think they'll dry out quite soon," he said worriedly, looking inside the box of matches. "They didn't have time to get ruined."

Dan's plan. Pathetic. "We haven't got time for your idea, Dan," I said.

"We've got to have more than your idea. Just talking to them!"

"Reasoning with them, not just talking. We do know quite a lot now. But we've got to start."

"And how do you do that?"

"Call them up," I said tautly. "Right now."

I went over to the blocked speaking tube. Dan darted in to get there first. He put his hand over it. "No. We're going to do my plan. We'll practise."

"What about John? How much time do we have?"

"We've got time, if they were telling us the truth."

"But you're the one who was so worried."

"We're going to practise my idea till we get it right. It could work, Mandy."

We argued some more. Dan was intractable and I had to let him have his way. I knew we had to present a united front to the ghosts. They would surely exploit any dissension we showed between ourselves.

He struck a match and the head was limp and fell off. "We'll wait, then – just a little," he said obdurately. "It's going to work."

We had to wait quite a while until the matches decided they were dry enough to work. Outside the rain died away, yet the thunder went on rolling around from time to time. Dan passed the time by laying out strands of cotton on the floor and picking the best colour for what he had in mind.

At last we started to rehearse the routine he had planned. With his penknife he cut one of the lemons in half and squeezed juice into the egg-cup. . .

It took several attempts and an age of time before he was satisfied. By the time he got to the last go it was dark outside. He said triumphantly, "See? It really works! And it's much better in the dark too, isn't it!"

"Keep your voice down," I hissed once again. But I had to admit that on this last try Dan's ludicrous scheme had begun to look just a little more credible.

"So, um, we're ready, then. . ." I said, suddenly overcome with nerves.

"Yup. You're going to do all the talking, right?"

"Yup."

"Well then. . ."

"Hey," I said, still putting off the evil moment, "Light a couple more of the candles – create an atmosphere. Yes?"

"Yeah – good idea!"

With four candles casting their light up from the floor, where Dan had stuck them in their own grease, the room looked and felt spooky enough to satisfy any ghost. I shivered as I went back to the speaking tube.

But then, we were both still very wet. I was shivering because of that, I told myself. *I will not be frightened, come what may.*

I took my socks out of the mouthpiece. They were dry and for one ridiculous instant I thought of putting them on again, but I didn't.

I was ready.

I cleared my throat and said hoarsely into the tube, "Hello. . .? We want to. . . we have to talk to you."

Silence. A little draught came through the tube and that was all. "You can hear me. I know you can. We want to talk to you."

The tube began to vibrate. I heard the man say, deeply, warmly, "You're back! How *nice.*"

The woman's voice was syrupy and deliberately musical and all the more alarming because of it. "Hello, Amanda," it cooed ever so gently. It made me shudder, hearing my name spoken like that.

"We're waiting," I said tremulously.

"Coming. . ." her voice sang, as in a game.

14

"Coming to get you. . ." the old voice carolled, sweeping down the corridor.

Dan and I waited. No time to change course now. No time to re-think our plans. This was it.

The door opened slowly at first, cautiously, then swung all the way back to the wall with a plaster-cracking bang.

"There you are!" The old man's voice said heartily.

"Come," the woman said, "Come and talk. . ." Her voice was already receding, going back whence it had come.

"No!" I called resolutely.

The voices came back. "You don't want to talk?" they said in unison, with a tone of surprise.

"No – we will talk to you," I said, "But in here."

A pause. A definite feeling of agitation outside the door. I felt cold and fearful and shivered, and bit my lip. Dan was behind me; I didn't look.

They had communicated with each other in this time. They spoke again as one voice, "It is forbidden!"

"We give you the right to come in," I insisted.

"It is not yours to give!" Now they were furious.

"It is. This is our house now and we make you welcome here."

"Do you welcome death?" the woman snarled. "Obey us!"

"We have so much to talk about," I said. "I know so many things now."

That hooked them. In the dim corridor I saw an oily bulking of the air as if they were edging forward to the doorway.

"What could *you* tell us?" the woman asked contemptuously.

At my feet was the copy of the *High Peak Journal*. I opened it out to show the picture of the croquet game.

"I can tell you one thing. You are not Mr and Mrs Jack Merriman. You're not them – you're not even old – so can you please drop that very silly pretence?"

I could feel a tugging at the magazine. I held on tight. The candle flames flickered in a little breeze. The tugging became stronger; I held on harder.

The breeze died down and the magazine was mine again.

As I had suggested to Dan, I had the suspicion that the ghosts were more powerful in some places than in others. My hope was that in here, "the forbidden room", they might be at their weakest.

I waited.

"What more have you to tell us?" the old man boomed. It was a bullying shout, empty of real threat.

"We don't say you're right," the woman added quickly.

"Well, come in, and you'll find out what I've got to tell you."

Dan added his bit. "We invite you in – so it's allowed."

There was a shimmering convulsion of almost-invisible form. The two apparitions were coiling into the room, distorting the air as they came. When they came to a stop there was only the occasional flux of oily colour to reveal their presence.

They were within four feet of me. Silent. Perhaps we were all holding our breath.

"You are the children of Mr John Armitage," I whispered to them. "He left you here and you died."

Now the silence was terrifying. I did not know how they were reacting.

I kept my voice low. "We know about you." I thought of a new angle: "We are sorry for you."

Not clever. They had no need to speak to manifest their anger. It filled the room.

I was losing it. Losing the battle before it had begun. "Look – listen to me," I said intensely, "We know you are very clever and very powerful. You don't have to pretend to be anything other than you are. Not with us. All right?"

Silence. That was something, anyway. I took a deep breath and let it out slowly. I put my hand on my chest, introducing myself formally as one might to a foreigner with very little English.

"I'm Amanda," I said. "That's Dan behind me. Who are you?"

Time passed. Not much.

A high voice said, very close, "I'm Grace, and he's Edward."

My mind whirred. How old was that voice? The person who possessed it was younger than me – that was certain. Younger than Dan, too. Must be. It was hard to tell, though, because the voice was so pure and the words were so precisely articulated.

I said quietly, "Hello, Grace, hello Edward," and went on as amicably as I could, "Let's all just settle down, shall we?"

I sat down on the floor, cross-legged. I couldn't tell what the ghosts were doing. I turned my head to Dan for a second. He looked tense, sitting there in his corner, waiting for the signal.

The initiative was mine now. "That's better," I said in a husky voice that was meant to sound hearty. "Now, Grace. Edward. We know that you want our father."

There was a sudden, swirly bulking of the air just in front of me. Another light, high child's voice said, "He's our father. He's not yours!"

"He promised," said the other small voice. The younger one, I thought. "When he went away he promised he would come back."

"We didn't want him to go."

"So he *promised*."

Ah. Well, obviously it was going to be too much to expect them to be reasonable. I asked courteously, "How old are you?"

There was a another little pause. "I'm ten and Grace is eight."

Much too much to expect them to be reasonable.

"And what exactly makes you think our father is your father, come back to you?"

I jumped a mile when the old man's voice came back in powerfully. "You know nothing! You wish us to reveal our secrets and you have nothing to offer in return!"

"So we'll hurt them then, shall we?" Grace said in her own voice, with no emotion whatsoever.

I tried to divert her. "How do you do that? The voices?"

Grace said uninterestedly, "Practice."

Edward was smug. "We practised on the silly people. We found out all sorts of things we could do."

Dan said, "You mean the people in the sanatorium?"

"It was good if you found one who could see you."

"They got so scared."

I was beginning to sort out which voice was which. Listening to these two unseen children talking to us in the candle-lit room was the oddest phenomenon of all so far. I was so curious I couldn't resist it. "And could you show yourselves to us, so we could see you?"

"We could to you. You have the gift."

"Your brother hasn't."

The old woman howled, "But you are trying to trick us! You are not nice! You will not see us!"

"We have been nice to you," Edward's voice hung in the air plaintively. "We have been good." The plaintive note was totally fake and he changed it, becoming at once subtly older and disturbingly aroused. "But you are not good and I think we should do things to you now."

"Look," I said quickly, "I know why you think John is your father and I know what really

165

happened to your own father. If you behave yourselves I'll tell you."

A silence answered that and I spoke into it quietly. "The first day we came here you got excited, didn't you, when John said about how he had come over from Australia. And our John even looks like your John."

"He is *our* father," Grace said passionately. "He is my Papa. He likes the same music. He likes us – but he can't see us, that's all."

I said slowly, one word at a time. "He is not your father."

Bad move.

"Anyway – you're not so clever!" Edward joined in at a high level of hysteria. "You think you're so clever – but you're not! You didn't find everything we put in the Ice House! You're not so clever!"

"You're not clever at all," Grace said viciously. "And you're a *liar*!"

"*Liar–liar–liar*!"

"*Fib–fib–liar*!"

They'd gone beyond my control: the window flew wide open and through it poured a hundred flitting, dodging black shapes which tore around our heads like tiny demons from hell.

"You don't like bats, do you?" One of the ghosts was laughing. It kept on laughing as it shouted, "We like them! They like us!"

The laughter became forced and underneath it I

heard the sound it was trying to hide. Dan, choking, on his back on the floor, holding his throat, with his eyes popping out of his head like white marbles.

The other ghost – I couldn't tell which when they were shouting – squeaked out, "Inside or outside, we have the craft!"

The bats flew faster and wilder, banging into my face as they passed by. The ghosts were both chanting now.

"Inside – outside!"

"Inside – *outside*!"

"Stop it!" I yelled over their chant. "If you don't stop it, you'll never know what happened to your father! Never! Dan knows it all – he could tell you!"

The chanting ceased in mid-word. Before another second had passed bats began darting out of the window, one by one, incredibly fast. The candles had not blown out: in fact, nearing the end of their natural lives, they were burning more brightly than ever, and by their light I could see Dan was recovering. He struggled to sit up, feeling his throat.

"I do know about your father. . ." I could hear anxiety in the bruised voice. Dan wanted to get on with it before the candles were exhausted. "He drowned at sea. . . He was on a ship called the *Waratah* and it went down off the coast of Africa. . . There were no survivors – not one!"

"No! He *promised*!" Edward shouted angrily.

"Father never lied to us!" Grace was just as ferocious.

They were moving into the manic state again. I bawled out desperately, "He couldn't help it! It wasn't his fault! He died!"

A hush descended after the shouting.

Edward remarked mournfully, "This was his room. He called it his sanctum. He smoked his pipe in here."

His sister sounded very solemn. "We were not allowed in because there are rules, even for people who love each other. He was nice and he promised to come back. We wouldn't let him go if he didn't."

"He wanted to come back." I picked up the sea-disasters book. "But it's in here in black and white. They all died."

Edward's voice was rich with excitement, "That's where you are mistaken. We know about the Waratah! We heard talk!"

Grace said shrilly, "There was a passenger who got off the ship because he knew it wasn't safe!"

"Yes – and that was our father! It could have been, you know!"

"Yes – and there are lions in Africa! And dangerous jungles too! He might have had difficulties trying to get back to us!"

"But he did and now he's here!"

"Oh for heaven's sake!" I was beside myself with

frustration. "Your father would be over a hundred years old if he was still alive! It's not *possible*."

They wouldn't take it in. Together they whispered musically, "He promised. . ."

These dead children were not logical. They were as mad as any of the patients in the old sanatorium. No point waiting any longer: Dan's crazy plan just had to work.

I said suddenly, "Wait – wait. . . I sense him! He is with us! Your father is here – with us! He needs to say something. . ."

Behind me Dan would be sitting with his arms crossed. He'd had his cue and about now he would start to move the hand that was hidden beneath the outer arm. Very slowly and surreptitiously.

"He cannot speak," I intoned like a medium at a seance, "But he is frantic to talk to you. . ." I made myself scream out, "Look!"

There, in the middle of the candles in the middle of the floor, the wooden dip pen was moving. It made its way jerkily over a sheet of the writing paper. Pulled by Dan on a length of grey cotton.

I was resigned to failure as I watched it travel over the paper in almost a dead straight line, well-nigh flat to the ground. No one could believe that it could be writing anything. Dan's stupid plan. . . What a silly idea it had been.

But there was utter quiet in the room, all the same.

The pen stopped moving. I went to it and looked at it, pretending to examine it. "No ink!" I cried – and threw the pen over to Dan as though in disgust, thus getting rid of the evidence.

"This is wrong," Grace's voice said doubtfully. "We would know if he was here."

"He was! I felt it! I have the gift, you know. . ." Now I had the piece of paper held up over one of the candles. I made like I was looking for words on the paper. "He had something to tell you. . ."

It took longer than it had when we practised, because I was nervous and did not want to hold the paper too near the candle flame. But the page was getting hot.

"Enough!" the old man's voice called, engorged with fury. The sound was *huge*.

"Wait!" I shouted back. "Look! Look!"

At last the words were beginning to appear. Large capitals. In a brownish colour, faint, but distinguishable. . .

"LISTEN TO THEM"

And that was it. Three words in magic writing, using lemon juice. It didn't show up till you heated it. A second-rate trick from Dan's big book of *Wonders*.

Dan's acting was pretty second-rate, too. He said excitedly, "He wants them to listen to us – and to what you're going to tell them! That's amazing!"

"I sense his sadness," I whispered, "How sad he is."

"We don't believe you," Grace said tightly.

"You don't have to. Though he wants you to – for your own sakes." I pointed to the book on the floor. "Can you read?"

"Yes," said Edward, "Of course we can!"

"It's all in there. The account of the *Waratah*." I peered at the book myself. "There *was* a passenger who got off, at Durban. And he had a name. It's printed right here. Claude Sawyer."

The air around me got very cold. It was like the ghosts had jostled in on me and I was *inside* them somehow while they were reading over my shoulder.

I drove the point home. "Not John Armitage. Someone called Sawyer. Your father doesn't want you distressing yourselves by waiting for him. He's not coming back. He can't."

Dan said, "You know that the man you have in that room is not your father."

The air became less dense around me and I was warmer. The ghosts had moved.

"No!" They cried in harmony.

A swift, straining, swooping sound and the air was clear of them altogether. They were back in the corridor.

We heard them as they rushed back to John's room.

"Not true!" they wailed. "Not true!"

15

"**D**id it work?" Dan asked in a whisper.

"I don't know. We're going to have to go after them."

"So. Let's go."

Still, we hesitated; in this room we had felt comparatively safe, but in other parts of the house...

All I said was, "Take a candle; it's dark."

We each took one of the guttering candles. I blew the others out and we left the sanctum.

The golden glow from the candles flickered on the hall walls as we went towards John's room. The door was shut. "We can't get in!" Dan groaned.

I reached out for the handle. It turned. The door opened.

Inside the only light was from the one big

standard lamp next to John. The light poured down on him as from a spotlight. He was exactly as we had seen him all those hours ago, but his head had drooped and his eyes were closed.

"Is he still all right?" Dan asked with terrible anxiety. "Are they here? Where are they?"

The corners of the room were pitch black, but I knew where the ghosts were. To me, the view we had of John was not as clear as it should be; his shape was blurred. The oily air clinging around him made me think of a family clustered around a sick pet. It was as if they were stroking his hair.

I said, "I hope you're saying goodbye."

They weren't listening. I had to get their attention. I walked towards John and reached through Grace and Edward to feel his neck. A vivid shiver ran up my back and I withdrew my hand. At least there had been a discernible pulse there.

"I suppose you know it's very wrong to kill someone," I said in a low voice. "Your father wouldn't approve."

They did not respond. I stepped back again. "But perhaps you've killed already. What happened to Miss Armitage – your aunt?"

Nothing.

"You killed her – didn't you?"

"No," Grace said softly. "We are good."

"It would not have been wrong to kill her,"

Edward explained, invisible, "Because she was bad."

"But we are good," they said together. It sounded exceptionally sinister.

I demanded to know. "How did she die then?"

"She became nervous. We teased her."

"She deserved it. She hated us."

They were speaking so fast it was impossible to tell which was which.

"She sold our father's piano. He loved to sing for us."

"She threw away the letters he sent us."

"She *said* it was a mistake – but she meant to do it."

"And there was only one left."

"He found it."

The oily colours were thicker. I could almost make out two distinct, small shapes; could actually see John's hair moving as they fondled it.

"He saved it from the flames."

"He is a good father."

"What about you," I asked, "How did you die?"

My heart vaulted up in my chest as a voice we had not heard before came shrieking from a distance. It was a woman's voice, calling harshly, excitedly, "That's it – that's it, Edward – save your sister – save Grace – *save her*!"

Edward said, "We drowned."

"In the lake."

"She saw us drown."

"We were scared."

"She was looking out of the window and she shouted. . ."

The woman's voice came in again just as before, as if on a recording, "That's it – that's it, Edward – save your sister – save Grace – *save her*!"

"She wanted us both to drown," the girl's voice said gravely. "It was her fault. So she drowned too. It was fair."

They laughed and Edward said, "She kept hearing voices. She wanted to get away from them. . . We watched. And were glad."

So. Grace and Edward lay somewhere deep beneath the surface of the boggy lake. Never found. Over the course of the many ensuing years they had developed their horrible skills while at the same time remaining the two children who had run wild.

I spoke very deliberately. "And would you now agree that John is not your father? Now your own father has guided you in this?"

It was the key moment – the all-important question. I had to wait some moments for a reply.

"He could still be our father – if he wanted to be," Grace said defiantly.

The question had been answered.

Close all avenues of escape. "Would you let him choose, then? Choose between you and us?"

They didn't answer that.

"He would choose us," I said with finality.

Dan stepped forward until he was by my side. "Your own father isn't coming back. Sometimes grown-ups can't keep their promises, even if they want to." He created a little pause. "You could. . . leave, couldn't you? If you weren't waiting for him to keep his promise?"

I admired that suggestion a lot and it clearly stopped the ghosts dead in their tracks. Only thing was . . . as far as I could tell, there was, suddenly, only one of them here now. . .

Grace said tentatively, "You mean . . . go further away? You mean – Out Away. . ."

"Don't you think," I suggested, "That your father might be waiting for you . . . out away?"

She laughed. High-pitched children's party laughter with that note of hysteria. Where was Edward?

"It's wide and dark. You don't know about it. It's big, the Out Away. There's a word you call it. . . 'Infinite'. When you go out away you can't get back. The Out Away, that's away for ever." She repeated, as in a frightened trance, "Out Away – Out Away – Away for ever. . ."

"I can't help that," I said distractedly. *Where was Edward?* "It's what you should do. Go 'Out Away'. Could you? Are you brave enough?"

Where was he? The little configuration of oily air that was Grace was shifting uneasily around John,

176

as though she was rocking herself back and forward in a state of excruciating unease. I felt a chilly draught – she said – "We *could*. . . Yes. . ." – and I was caught by an enormous force and swept into the air – rushed to John's side. Pieces of paper drifted down around me and one set itself square on the desk. The wooden dip pen floated down slowly and came to rest on the paper.

"Get him back!" Edward commanded in my ear.

I couldn't move. My arms were pinioned to my sides by his colossal strength. I stuttered, "I can't. . . I can't. . . It was *his* choice – not mine!"

'He will write to us again! Get him back! *Now.*"

Grace observed without curiosity, "There's a piece of cotton on that pen."

Oh no.

Again the pen moved across the paper. Then it rose up in the air, dangling questioningly on its cotton thread.

Everything started to quiver like an earthquake was coming. Out of the corner of my eye I saw John slump from his chair to the floor – I couldn't see what was happening to Dan. We passed each other in the air, hurled with sickening force right across the room and slamming into the walls.

My elbow felt as if it was broken and the pain made me cry out as I sagged forward on to my knees. Across the room Dan came to his feet, winded, all bent over and gasping for breath.

The old man's voice resounded mightily through the room. "Fakes and liars! DECEIVERS!"

I raised my head and sobbed, "Us? *Us* deceivers? What about you? Telling yourselves our father is yours! What about you?"

Dan gasped, "You're playing games with someone who doesn't belong to you!"

Desperation gave me the strength to get up. "*Listen*! Your own father is not coming back! Face it! In fact, he might even be cross with you for staying here – just because you're scared! That's the only reason you're still here, isn't it? You're scared!"

They were insulted and spoke as one, angrily, "*No*!"

I drove onwards. "You're not meant to be here – you know it!"

"I'm going to put this pen right through your lying tongue," Edward exulted savagely and the pen sprang into an upright position, poised like a knife.

His voice became thick and wet, clotted with anticipation, "Then I'll kill you both in an exciting way."

"And I'll help you!" Grace added happily, as if they were going to make a cake together.

I had no more to fight with. Bruised to the bone, I felt I might die of weariness anyway, before the pen got to me. I said faintly, "Well, isn't it lucky your father isn't with us after all. If he could hear you now. . . If he could *see* you, killing some other father's children. . ." Then the words I dimly imagined would be the last I ever spoke arrived from somewhere of their own accord: "He wouldn't want to keep his promise after that."

The pen was still poised. Everything was just as it had been. Only something had changed. . . I just kept rambling on in the same tired way.

"You can't make something true by wanting it. . . Our mother died. I'd like her back, but it's not going to happen. . . Then we were getting used to having a father. . . it was good. Well, you remember what it was like when you were here with your own father. All that time ago. . . Can't you just get quiet and remember him and think what he'd really want for you and what he'd really want *from* you, because he loved you. . ."

The room became deathly quiet and seemed to get quieter still, second by second. "Ask yourselves that," I whispered.

The pen dropped to the floor.

"Don't know. . ." said a small voice, and I could imagine Edward's bottom lip trembling as he spoke.

Grace said to her brother, "They want us to go Out Away, Edward!" And she was *scared*.

"Oh . . . but . . . we can't do that. It's. . ." The contemplation of that course of action had its effect on Edward, too.

"Look," I said, and I had to battle to keep life out of my voice, "All we want for you is what your father would want for you. Personally, I don't care – I really don't. Just think about it."

They thought about it. And thought about it. You could almost hear them thinking. And then communicating, silently. And then they said as one, slightly wheedling, "If we *did* go. . ."

"Yes?"

"If we *did* go, we wouldn't really want to go alone, if we could help it. . ."

I was ahead of Dan here and I was alarmed. But Dan said sympathetically, "I know. I'm sorry."

Edward put on a charming little voice when he asked, "What about you? Would you come with us?"

I was appalled. Grace loved the idea and put on her prettiest voice too. "We wouldn't be horrid to you ever again. We could have fun . . . somewhere. It wouldn't be painful for you."

Absolutely not, I thought. There was a surge of oily oncoming air and I felt a polite constriction starting around my neck.

I was still able to speak so far and through my terror I was polite but firm, though my voice sounded squashed. "It's very kind of you to ask us, but I think there's an order to things, somehow, and we all have to be where we're supposed to be."

Dan backed me up ardently. "She's right. You know she is."

The pressure was taken off my neck. "You're being nasty to us," Edward said darkly. "Very nasty. . ."

There was a puff of wind and he had vanished from my side. I couldn't see where Grace was, either. Dan looked at me, aware that something had taken place; I held up a hand to stop him speaking. They hadn't gone. Where would they be? In one of the dark corners, no doubt. I felt my elbow and winced. But it seemed it wasn't broken, and that was something.

They were having one of their conferences, I guessed. There was no knowing what this colloquy would produce; over the many years their sense of morality had . . . well . . . decomposed with their bodies in the lake.

Dan again wanted to say something. Again I stopped him. We limped haltingly a little way across the room until we were closer together. We would wait here, appearing patient and confident. We had done all we could do and now it was out of our hands.

After what seemed like several hours, but was more probably a minute or two, it was Edward who announced the result of their consultation.

His voice came from the furthest corner. Dignified, but with a residue of hurt in it still.

"Do you think you could possibly open a window for us?"

My heart began to bump with excitement and relief. The thumping of it made my ears ring and I wasn't sure if someone – Grace, probably – was sniffling in their corner.

Too bad if she was. With Dan I walked stiffly to a window. We opened the wooden shutters.

We unlocked and raised the window. The dark air outside was not cold, but was appreciably cooler than it was in here.

They were by our side. We backed off from the window.

Grace was bitter. "You shouldn't have come here. None of you."

"It's not fair," Edward said, using the archetypal phrase of childhood, and I felt their cold breath in my ear as they repeated it together loudly and vehemently.

"Not fair – it's not *fair*!"

Dan said quietly, "Perhaps not. But right."

He was being very honest and I think that finally did it for us.

We stood there feeling colder and colder and eventually Edward's voice said sulkily, "We're going now."

There was a pause. They hadn't gone.

Grace said primly, "I don't think you've been very nice."

And at last there was a growing, sucking sound, a whirlpool of speeding air, a twister, a tornado right next to me. Dan felt it too; I could feel him trembling.

You couldn't hear them at all well in the midst of their hurricane.

Edward said faintly, "It's happening. . ."

"That was quick." Grace.

"I'm scared."

"So am I."

"Never mind, Grace." He was the big brother with his little sister. Comforting her. The wind grew stronger still and I drew Dan to me and we held on to each other in case we should be dragged through the window too. The room was wild with tearing air and the whole house creaked and shook as if it would uproot itself and fly. We sank to our knees and held on to each other tighter.

I heard Grace cry out, near the end, as the twisting wind was being pulled through the open window, "Can't we change our minds? I wish you would come too. . . Ohhhh. . .!"

And the wind vanished, sucked into the wide open spaces outside. Was gone, as though at once dispersed when out of Lowlake.

An afterdraft gusted back into the room.

With it came the echo of a childish giggle.

We got to our feet in the ruined room and stood there by the open window, Dan and me. The atmosphere was sombre and all I felt was a kind of emptiness.

John was still collapsed on the floor and for a moment I was unable to move towards him because I thought the ghosts might have killed him. . . Then he stirred and sighed to himself and said, "Oh my word. . ." and we went rushing over to him.

"You're all right!" Dan discovered with fierce joy.

"What – uh – what time is it?" He was confused, but it was our John, returned to us. He looked down at his clothes. "What am I wearing?"

Dan was hugging him now. "You're all right!"

I was babbling and hugging too. "We thought you were going to die. . ."

"Die? Die? Let me. . ."

He struggled to his feet, with Dan and me still still clinging to him as if he were a fireman taking us from a burning building. He had lost none of his strength – he was himself, through and through.

"The house. . ." he said.

"Yes, John?" I answered dutifully.

"It's the house. You were right. How could I have. . .?"

"It doesn't matter – not now!" Dan yelled through a face-splitting grin.

"No. It does. . . It was – I was – Oh Lord. . ."

He was remembering something.

The military manner came back to him, almost audibly snapping back into place. "We're not staying here a moment longer! Not one second longer than we have to!"

It was wonderful. He was wonderful – so gloriously business-like – John-like – the John we knew and cherished. He didn't want to talk; he wanted to act. He had failed us in some way he couldn't yet understand, but it would never happen again and the prime objective now was a tactical withdrawal from Lowlake, to be carried out at speed. He gave his orders rapidly. We were leaving right now, so we must take with us only what was essential – we would pack some food and camp out under the stars as we had before.

"Now let's get started!"

In the event, our preparations took longer than he had planned, because Dan's idea of essentials included everything electronic. The old book for boys was the one exception. His relief at having John back, and his pride in his own part in achieving that, was so great that he was incapable of feeling the still-present menace of Lowlake. For him, the house was now a simple arrangement of bricks and mortar as described by Mr Burton.

I had my doubts there. And, for all his apparent confidence, so did John. He was the one who went round the house turning on all the lights. As if, I thought, that would do any good.

While John and Dan stuck together in everything they did, I did my own thing. Packing more quickly than carefully, I was ready within minutes. I needed a little time to myself for something I had to do.

"There's nothing but baked beans!" John was saying, amazed. "And what hit this place?"

He was in the kitchen with Dan – looking quite wonderful in his own clothes. I kept quiet and left them to it. I got my torch and went outside.

The spade we had used was still there where we had left it, abandoned on the spot when Dan cut himself. Or had been cut? It didn't matter now.

You're not so clever. You didn't find everything we put in the Ice House.

I dug. Under the flagstone we had removed.

Dan and John were calling for me from the house by the time I hit the tin. It was a biscuit tin, rusting, with parading soldiers pictured on it. They had buried it deep.

There wasn't much inside. Just a piece of paper. I shone the torch on it. I had to know, after what Edward had said in the sanctum, what it was we had failed to find.

There was a drawing in pencil. Carefully executed but undeniably childish. You could guess that the middle figure was meant to be a man, a handsome, well-dressed man, and that the smaller figures holding his hand on either side of him were his children, a boy and a girl.

The writing, in ink, was uneven and childish too. Above the man it said, "*PAPA*" and under the picture there were a few more words.

They read, "*We love you so.*"

That was all. The whole secret.

Emotion filled my throat and in my eyes was a little acid burst of forming tears.

As the first tear started its downward run I turned my head a little to brush away the wetness, and caught a glimpse of a small buckled shoe and a pale woollen stocking.

The leg stepped back into the darkness.

Ah. Grace.

I willed myself to keep my eyes only on what I was doing.

With enormous care I replaced the drawing in the tin and the tin in the ground, and reburied it deep.

Getting to my feet, I shone the torch on the ground on my way back to the garden wall, which I climbed with my eyes fixed on my own hands, and I kept my head down all the way to the house, controlling the almost irresistible urge to look around.

Please God let me make it out of this place before I start them up again.

As I went inside I called out brightly, "I really think we should go as soon as possible!"

* * *

I made it out of Lowlake. We all made it out, sitting together in the front of the Landrover so each one of us was continuously touching another member of the family.

The headlights swept along the lonely road steadily and the miles were adding up and we were fine.

Dan even managed to fall asleep, curled around the gear stick and resting on John, who drove carefully with one arm around him.

John looked across at me and smiled. About Dan being asleep.

We were coming down a long incline, way past Essop already, leaving the Peaks. John cut the noisy engine and we coasted slowly and silently. He wanted to talk and, as usual with John, he didn't know quite what to say.

"You OK?" he asked. I had waited quite a while before he even said that.

"Yes."

"Sure?"

"Sure. And, um, John. . ."

"Yes?"

"I'm glad you're back with us."

"Back . . . yes." There was understanding in his face at that moment. He said, "Mandy. . ."

And I said, "Yes, John?"

"This . . . 'John' business."

"Yes?"

"I am your father. I like being your father."

"Oh. That's good."

He said shyly, "So I think, from now on, it's 'Dad'. If you like."

I did.

The Landrover rattled onwards and I thought about Grace and Edward.

I'd seen them before we left. It had been, I thought, a mark of respect on their part.

We had been about to go – about to take our flight from Lowlake. The Landrover was packed and whatever was left was left to rot. The lights John had switched on would fail, one by one; gradually the roof would let in water again.

Dan and John were already together in the front of the jeep. I had let them get in first because in my own mind I was their guardian till we got safely away.

I had my hand on the open car door and I turned back to the house. You do this. You say, I'll just fix this picture in my memory and then I can go.

There they were. Grace and Edward. Standing under the light over the front door.

Dan and John didn't see them. I snatched a glance to check and though John was looking at me he saw nothing – he was fine – oblivious.

But I saw them. Beyond question. There they were . . . about a foot apart from one another, heads up, looking straight at us. Grace had a sort of lacey, creamy dress on and Edward was wearing a sailor suit. They were standing there in the yellow electric light and they were looking at us. No emotion, no animation at all in their dark eyes. Two very elderly children who had moved far beyond being human.

At the time I remember thinking *aren't they small* and that was all. Then John and Dan were saying things like, "Well come on, then!" and it was time to go; I looked away and when I looked back they weren't there. But I saw them. I know I did . . .

I'd guessed they wouldn't really leave. They would never leave. They tricked us just like we tricked them with the magic writing. But I don't know exactly why they were tied to the old house in the hollow. It might have been that they were scared of change, or of the unknown; it might have been – well – it might have been for any number of reasons. I'll never be certain about it.

But of all the reasons I can think of, one seems most likely, knowing Grace and Edward as I had come to.

They were still waiting for their father.

After all, he had promised.